Hepsey Burke

Frank N. Westcott

Illustrated by Frederick R. Gruger

"YOU HAVEN'T SEEN ANYTHING THAT LOOKED LIKE A PARSON, HAVE YOU? YOU CAN GENERALLY SPOT 'EM EVERY TIME"

HEPSEY BURKE

BY
FRANK N. WESTCOTT

ILLUSTRATED BY
FREDERICK R. GRUGER

1914

CONTENTS.

ILLUSTRATIONS.

"You haven't seen anything that looked like a parson, have you? You can generally spot 'em every time"

"I'm blessed if you 'aint sewin' white buttons on with black thread. Is anybody dead in the family, or 'aint you feelin' well this mornin'?"

"Nicholas Burke, what in the name of conscience does all this idiotic performance mean, I'd like to know?"

"Oh well, I always believe that two young married people should start out by themselves, and then if they get into a family row it won't scandalize the parish"

"I 'aint a chicken no more, Mrs. Betty, and I've 'most forgot how to do a bit of courtin'"

"I consider it a shame and a disgrace to the parish to have our rector in filthy clothes, drawing stone with a lot of ruffians"

"I've got a hunch, Sylvester Bascom, that it'll be you that'll have the last word, after all"

"Hepsey Burke, for all your molasses and the little bit of vinegar you say you keep by you, 'There are no flies on you' as Nickey would put it"

CHAPTER I

HEPSEY BURKE

The noisy, loose-jointed train pulled out of the station, leaving behind it a solitary young man, enveloped in smoke and cinders. In the middle of the platform stood a little building with a curb roof, pointed at both ends like a Noah's Ark; and the visitor felt that if he could only manage to lift up one side of the roof he would find the animals "two by two," together with the cylindrical Noah and the rest of his family. There was no one in sight but the station-master, who called out from the ticket office:

"Did you want to go to the village? The 'bus won't be down till the next train: but maybe you can ride up on the ice wagon."

"Thanks," the stranger replied. "I think I'll wait for the 'bus, if it's not too long."

"Twenty minutes or so, if Sam don't have to collect the passengers goin' West, and wait for a lot o' women that forget their handbags and have to get out and go back after 'em."

The new arrival was good to look at—a handsome, well-built fellow of about twenty-five, dressed in a gray suit which was non-committal as to his profession, with a clean-shaven face which bore the unmistakable stamp of good breeding and unlimited good-nature. He tilted his suit-case on end and sat down on it; then he filled his briar pipe, crossed his legs, and looked about to take stock of the situation. He gazed about curiously; but there was nothing of any special interest in sight, except, painfully conspicuous on the face of a grass terrace, the name of the village picked out in large letters composed of oyster-shells and the bottoms of protruding beer bottles stuck in the ground. The stranger found himself wondering where a sufficient number of bottles could be found to complete such an elaborate pattern. The only other marked feature of the landscape in the way of artistic decoration was the corrugated base of an old stove, painted white, which served as a flower vase. From this grew a huge bunch of scarlet geraniums, staring defiantly, and seeming fairly to sizzle in the hot, vibrant atmosphere, which was as still as the calm of a moon-lit night.

As the man on the suit-case gazed about him at the general air of dilapidation and neglect characteristic of a country town on the down grade, and recalled the congenial life of the city which he had left, with all its busy competition, with all its absorbing activities, the companionship of the men he loved, and the restful, inspiring intimacy with a certain young woman, he felt, for the moment, a pang of homesickness. If the station were a sample of the village itself, then life in such a place must be deadening to every finer sensibility and ambition; it must throw a man back on himself and make him morbid.

The momentary depression was relieved by the station-master, who suddenly appeared at the door of the Ark and called out:

"Here comes Hepsey Burke. Maybe she'll take you up; that'll be a dum sight more comfortable than Lipkin's 'bus."

There was nothing to be seen but a cloud of dust, advancing with the rapidity of a whirlwind along the highway, from which there gradually emerged a team and a "democrat," containing a woman, a boy about fourteen, and a middle-aged man.

As the turn-out drew up, the man took the reins from Mrs. Burke, who jumped out of the wagon with remarkable agility for one of her size and years, and, nodding to the station-master, came on to the platform.

Hepsey Burke was rather stout; and the lines from her nose to the corners of her mouth, and the wisps of gray hair which had blown about her face, indicated that she had passed the meridian of life. At first glance there was nothing striking about her appearance; but there was a subtle expression about the mouth, a twinkle about the large gray eyes behind the glasses she wore, that indicated a sense of humor which had probably been a God-send to her. She was strong and well, and carried with her an air of indomitable conviction that things worked themselves out all right in the long run.

The boy was obviously her son, and in spite of his overalls and frayed straw hat, he was a handsome little chap. He looked at you shyly from under a crop of curly hair, with half closed eyes, giving you the impression that you were being "sized up" by a very discriminating individual; and when he smiled, as he did frequently, he revealed a set of very white and perfect teeth. When he was silent, there was a little lifting of the inner brow which gave him a thoughtful look quite beyond his years; and you were sadly mistaken if you imagined that you could form a correct impression of Nicholas Burke at the first interview.

The man wore a sandy beard, but no mustache, and had a downcast, meekly submissive air, probably the depressing effect of many years of severe domestic discipline.

Mrs. Burke was evidently surprised to find no one there but the man on the suit-case; but as he rose and lifted his hat, she hesitated a moment, exclaiming:

"I beg pardon, but I was lookin' for a parson who was to arrive on this train. You haven't seen anything that looked like a parson, have you? You can generally spot 'em every time."

The young man smiled.

"Well, no; I seem to be the only passenger who got off the train; and though I'm a clergyman, you don't seem to find it easy to 'spot' me."

Mrs. Burke, with a characteristic gesture, pulled her glasses forward with a jerk and settled them firmly back again on the bridge of her nose. She surveyed the speaker critically as she questioned:

"But you don't seem to show the usual symptoms—collar buttoned behind, and all that."

"I am sorry to disappoint you, Madam, but I never travel in clerical uniform. Can't afford it."

"Well, you've got more sense than most parsons, if I may say so. Maybe you're the one I'm lookin' for: Mr. Donald Maxwell."

"That is my name, and I am sure you must be Mrs. Burke."

"Sure thing!"—shaking his outstretched hand heartily. "Now you come right along with me, Mr. Maxwell, and get into the democrat and make yourself comfortable." They walked round to the front of the station. "This, Mr. Maxwell, is Jonathan Jackson, the Junior Warden; and this is my son Nicholas, generally known as Nickey, except when I am about to spank him. Say, Jonathan, you just h'ist that trunk into the back of the wagon, and Nickey, you take the parson's suit-case."

The Junior Warden grinned good-naturedly as he shook hands with the new arrival. But Hepsey continued briskly: "Now, Jonathan, you get into the back seat with Nickey, and Mr. Maxwell, you sit with me on the front seat so that I can talk to you. Jonathan means well, but his talk's limited to crops and symptoms, even if he is an old friend, my next door neighbor, and the Junior Warden."

Jonathan obeyed orders; and, as he got into the wagon, winked at Maxwell and remarked:

"You see we have to take a back seat when Hepsey drives; and we have to hold on with both hands. She's a pacer."

"Don't you let him frighten you, Mr. Maxwell," Hepsey replied. "Jonathan would probably hold on with both hands if he lay flat on his back in a ten-acre lot. He's just that fearless and enterprisin'."

Then, starting the horses with a cluck, she turned to Maxwell and continued:

"I guess I didn't tell you I was glad to see you; but I am. I got your note tellin' me when you were comin', but I didn't get down to the

4

station in time, as the men are killin' hogs to-day, and until I get the in'ards off my hands, I haven't time for anything."

"I am sorry to have put you to the trouble of coming at all. I'm sure it's very good of you."

"No trouble; not the least. I generally look after the visitin' parsons, and I'm quite used to it. You can get used to 'most anything."

Maxwell laughed as he responded:

"You speak as if it weren't always a pleasure, Mrs. Burke."

"Well, I must admit that there are parsons and parsons. They are pretty much of a lottery, and it is generally my luck to draw blanks. But don't you worry about that; you don't look a bit like a parson."

"I think that's a rather doubtful compliment."

"Oh, well, you know what I mean. There are three kinds of people in the world; men, women, and parsons; and I like a parson who is a man first, and a parson afterwards; not one who is a parson first, and a man two weeks Tuesday come Michaelmas."

Donald laughed: he felt sure he was going to make friends with this shrewd yet open-hearted member of his flock. The pace slackened as the road began a steep ascent. Mrs. Burke let the horses walk up the hill, the slackened reins held in one hand; in the other lolled the whip, which now and then she raised, tightening her grasp upon it as if for use, on second thoughts dropping it to idleness again and clucking to the horses instead. It was typical of her character—the means of chastisement held handy, but in reserve, and usually displaced by other methods of suasion.

As they turned down over the brow of the hill they drove rapidly, and as the splendid landscape of rolling country, tilled fields and pasture, stretching on to distant wooded mountains, spread out before him, Maxwell exclaimed enthusiastically, drawing a deep breath of the exhilarating air:

"How beautiful it is up here! You must have a delightful climate."

"Well," she replied, "I don't know as we have much climate to speak of. We have just a job lot of weather, and we take it regular—once after each meal, once before goin' to bed, and repeat if necessary before mornin'. I won't say but it's pretty good medicine, at that. There'd be no show for the doctor, if it wasn't fashionable to invite him in at the beginnin' and the end of things."

Jonathan, who up to this time had been silent, felt it incumbent to break into the conversation a bit, and interposed:

"I suppose you've never been up in these parts before?"

"No," Maxwell responded; "but I've always intended to come up during the season for a little hunting some time. Was there much sport last year?"

"Well, I can't say as there was, and I can't say *as* there wasn't. The most I recollect was that two city fellers shot a guide and another feller. But then it was a poor season last fall, anyway."

Maxwell gave the Junior Warden a quick look, but there was not a trace of a smile on his face, and Hepsey chuckled. Keeping her eyes on the horses as they trotted along at a smart pace over a road none too smooth for comfortable riding, she remarked casually:

"I suppose the Bishop told you what we wanted in the shape of a parson, didn't he?"

"Well, he hinted a few things."

"Yes; we're awful modest, like most country parishes that don't pay their rector more than enough to get his collars laundered. We want a man who can preach like the Archbishop of Canterbury, and call on everybody twice a week, and know just when anyone is sick without bein' told a word about it. He's got to be an awful good mixer, to draw the young people like a porous plaster, and fill the pews. He must have lots of sociables, and fairs, and things to take the place of religion; and he must dress well, and live like a gentleman on the salary of a book-agent. But if he brings city ways along with him and makes us feel like hayseeds, he won't be popular."

"That's a rather large contract!" Maxwell replied with a smile.

"Yes, but think what we're goin' to pay you: six hundred dollars a year, and you'll have to raise most of it yourself, just for the fun of it."

At this point the Junior Warden interrupted:

"Now, Hepsey, what's the use of upsettin' the young man at the start. He's—"

"Never mind, Jonathan. I'm tellin' the truth, anyway. You see," she continued, "most people think piety's at a low ebb unless we're gettin' up some kind of a holy show all the time, to bring people together that wouldn't meet anywhere else if they saw each other first. Then when they've bought a chance on a pieced bed-quilt, or paid for chicken-pie at a church supper, they go home feelin' real religious, believin' that if there's any obligation between them and heaven, it isn't on their side, anyway. Do you think you're goin' to fill the bill, Mr. Maxwell?"

"Well, I don't know," said Maxwell. "Of course I might find myself possessed of a talent for inventing new and original entertainments each week; but I'm afraid that you're a bit pessimistic, Mrs. Burke, aren't you?"

"No, I'm not. There's a mighty fine side to life in a country parish sometimes, where the right sort of a man is in charge. The people take him as one of their family, you know, and borrow eggs of his wife as easy as of their next door neighbor. But the young reverends expect too much of a country parish, and break their hearts sometimes because they can't make us tough old critters all over while you wait. Poor things! I'm sorry for the average country parson, and a lot sorrier for his wife."

"Well, don't you worry about me; I'm well and strong, and equal to anything, I imagine. I don't believe in taking life too seriously; it's bad for the nerves and digestion. It will be an entirely new experience for me, and I'm sure I shall find the people interesting."

"Yes, but what if they aren't your kind? I suppose you might find hippopotamuses interestin' for a while, but that's no reason you should like to live with 'em. Anyway, don't mind what people say. They aint got nothin' to think about, so they make up by talkin' about it, especially when it happens to be a new parson. We've been havin' odds and ends of parsons from the remnant counter now for six months or more; and that's enough to kill any parish. I believe that if the angel Gabriel should preach for us, half the congregation would object to the cut of his wings, and the other half to the fit of his halo. We call for all the virtues of heaven, and expect to get 'em for seven-forty-nine."

"Well—I shall have to look to you and the Wardens to help me out," he said. "You must help me run things, until I know the ropes."

"Oh! Bascom will run things for you, if you let him do the runnin'," she replied, cracking her whip. "You'll need to get popular first with him and his—then you'll have it easy."

Maxwell pondered these local words of wisdom, and recalled the Bishop's warning that Bascom, the Senior Warden, had not made life easy for his predecessors, and his superior's exhortation to firmness and tact, to the end that he, Maxwell, should hold his own, while taking his Senior Warden along with him. The Senior Warden was evidently a power in the land.

They had driven about a mile and a half when the wagon turned off the road, and drew up by a house standing some distance back from it; getting down, Mrs. Burke exclaimed:

"Welcome to Thunder Cliff, Mr. Maxwell. Thunder Cliff's the name of the place, you know. All the summer visitors in Durford have names for their houses; so I thought I'd call my place Thunder Cliff, just to be in the style."

Jonathan Jackson, who had kept a discreet silence during Hepsey's pointers concerning his colleague, the Senior Warden, interjected:

"There 'aint no cliff, Hepsey, and you know it. I always tell her, Mr. Maxwell, 'taint appropriate a bit."

"Jonathan, you 'aint no Englishman, and there's no use pretendin' that you are. Some day when I have a couple of hours to myself, I'll explain the whole matter to you. There isn't any cliff, and the house wants paintin' and looks like thunder. Isn't that reason enough to go on with? Now, Mr. Maxwell, you come in and make yourself perfectly at home."

CHAPTER II
GOSSIP

That afternoon Maxwell occupied himself in unpacking his trunks and arranging his room. As the finishing touch, he drew out of a leather case an exquisite miniature of a beautiful girl, which he placed on the mantelpiece, and at which he gazed for a long time with a wistful light in his fine gray eyes. Then he threw himself on the lounge, and pulling a letter from his inner pocket, read:

"Don't worry about expenses, dear. Six hundred is quite enough for two; we shall be passing rich! You must remember that, although I am a 'college girl,' I am not a helpless, extravagant creature, and I know how to economize. I am sure we shall be able to make both ends meet. With a small house, rent free, a bit of ground for a vegetable garden, and plenty of fresh air, we can accomplish almost anything, and be supremely happy together. And then, when you win advancement, as of course you will very soon, we shall appreciate the comforts all the more from the fact that we were obliged to live the simple life for a while.

"You can't possibly imagine how I miss you, sweetheart. Do write as soon as possible and tell me all about Durford. If I could just have one glimpse of you in your new quarters—but that would only be a wretched aggravation; so I keep saying to myself 'Some day, some day,' and try to be patient. God bless you and good-by."

Donald folded the letter carefully, kissed it, and tucked it away in his pocket. Clasping his hands behind his head, he gazed at the ceiling.

"I wonder if I'd better tell Mrs. Burke about Betty. I don't care to pass myself off as a free man in a parish like this. And yet, after all, it's none of their business at present. I think I'd better wait and find out if there's any possibility of making her happy here."

There was a knock at the door.

"Talk of angels," murmured Maxwell, and hurriedly returned the miniature to its case before opening the door to Mrs. Burke, who came to offer assistance.

"Don't bother to fuss for me," she said as he hastened to remove some books and clothes from a chair, so that she might sit down. "I only came up for a moment to see if there was anything I could do. Think you can make yourself pretty comfortable here? I call this room 'the prophet's chamber,' you know, because it's where I always put the visitin' parsons."

"They're lucky," he replied. "This room is just delightful with that jolly old fireplace, its big dormer windows, and the view over the river and the hills beyond: I shall be very comfortable."

"Well, I hope so. You know I don't think any livin'-room is complete without a fireplace. Next to an old friend, a bright wood fire's the best thing I know to keep one from getting lonesome."

"Yes—that and a good cigar."

"Well, I haven't smoked in some time now," Mrs. Burke replied, smiling, "so I can't say. What a lot of things you've got!"

"Yes, more than I thought I had."

"I do love to see a man tryin' to put things to rights. He never knows where anything belongs. What an awful lot of books you've got! I suppose you're just chuck full of learnin', clean up to your back teeth; but we won't any of us know the difference. Most city parsons preach about things that are ten miles over the heads of us country people. You can't imagine how little thinkin' most of us do up here.

We're more troubled with potato bugs than we are with doubts; and you'll have to learn a lot about us before you really get down to business, I guess."

"Yes, I expect to learn more from you than you will from me. That's one of the reasons why I wanted to come so far out in the country."

"Hm! I hope you won't be disappointed."

Mrs. Burke adjusted her glasses and gazed interestedly about the room at some pictures and decorations which Maxwell had placed in position, and inquired:

"Who is the plaster lady and gentleman standin' on the mantelpiece?"

"The Venus de Milo, and the Hermes of Praxiteles."

"Well, you know, I just can't help preferrin' ladies and gentlemen with arms and legs, myself. I suppose it's real cultivated to learn to like parts of people done in marble. Maybe when I go down to the city next fall to buy my trousseau, I'll buy a few plasters myself, to make the house look more cheerful-like."

Maxwell caught at the word "trousseau," and as Mrs. Burke had spoken quite seriously he asked:

"Are you going to be married, Mrs. Burke?"

"No such thing! But when a handsome young widow like me lives alone, frisky and sixty-ish, with six lonesome, awkward widowers in the same school district, you can never tell what might happen any minute; 'In time of peace prepare for war,' as the paper says."

Maxwell laughed reassuringly.

"I don't see why you laugh," Mrs. Burke responded, chuckling to herself. "'Taint polite to look surprised when a woman says she's a-goin' to get married. Every woman under ninety-eight has expectations. While there's life there's hope that some man will make a fool of himself. But unless I miss my guess, you don't catch me surrenderin' my independence. As long as I have enough to eat and am well, I'm contented."

"You certainly look the picture of health, Mrs. Burke."

"Oh, yes! as well as could be expected, when I'm just recoverin' from a visit from Mary Sam."

"What sort of a visitor is that?" asked Maxwell, laughing.

"Mary Sam is my sister-in-law. She spends a month with me every year on her own invitation. She is what you'd call a hardy annual. She is the most stingy and narrow-minded woman I ever saw. The bark on the trees hangs in double box-plaits as compared with Mary Sam. But I got the best of her last year. While I was cleanin' the attic I came across the red pasteboard sign with 'Scarlet Fever' painted on it, that the Board of Health put on the house when Nickey had the fever three years ago. The very next day I was watchin' the 'bus comin' up Main Street, when I saw Mary Sam's solferino bonnet bobbin' up and down inside. Before she got to the house, I sneaked out and pinned up the sign, right by the front door. She got onto the piazza, bag, baggage, and brown paper bundles, before she caught sight of it. Then I wish you could have seen her face: I wouldn't have believed so much could be done with so few features."

"She didn't linger long?" laughed the parson, who continued arranging his books while his visitor chatted.

"Linger? Well, not exactly. She turned tail and run lickety-spindle back for the 'bus as if she had caught sight of a subscription paper for foreign missions. I heard Jim Anderson, who drives the 'bus, snicker as he helped her in again; but he didn't give me away. Jim and I are good friends. But when she got home she wrote to Sally Ramsdale to ask how Nickey was; and Sally, not bein' on to the game, wrote back that there was nothin' the matter with Nickey that she knew of. Then Mary Sam wrote me the impudentest letter I ever got; and she came right back, and stayed two months instead of one, just to be mean. But that sign's done good service since. I've scared off agents and tramps by the score. I always hang it in the parlor window when I'm away from home."

13

"But suppose your house caught fire while you were away?"

"Well, I've thought of that; but there's worse things than fire if your insurance is all right."

Mrs. Burke relapsed into silence for a while, until Maxwell opened a box of embroidered stoles, which he spread out on the bed for her inspection.

"My! but aren't those beautiful! I never saw the like before. Where did you get 'em?"

"They were made by the 'Sisters of St. Paul' in Boston."

Hepsey gazed at the stoles a long time in silence, handling them daintily; then she remarked:

"I used to embroider some myself. Would you like to see some of it?"

"Certainly, I should be delighted to see it," Donald responded; and Mrs. Burke went in search of her work.

Presently she returned and showed Maxwell a sample of her skill—doubtless intended for a cushion-cover. To be sure it was a bit angular and impressionistic. Like Browning's poems and Turner's pictures, it left interesting room for speculation. To begin with, there was a dear little pink dog in the foreground, having convulsions on purple grass. In the middle-distance was a lay-figure in orange, picking scarlet apples from what appeared to be a revolving clothes-horse blossoming profusely at the ends of each beam. A little blue brook gurgled merrily up the hill, and disappeared down the other side only to reappear again as a blue streak in an otherwise crushed-strawberry sky. A pumpkin sun was disappearing behind emerald hills, shooting up equidistant yellow rays, like the spokes of a cart-wheel. Underneath this striking composition was embroidered the dubious sentiment "There is no place like home."

Maxwell examined carefully the square of cross-stitch wool embroidery, biting his lip; while Hepsey watched him narrowly, chuckling quietly to herself. Then she laughed heartily, and asked:

"Confess now; don't you think it's beautiful?"

Donald smiled broadly as he replied:

"It's really quite wonderful. Did you do it yourself?"

"To be sure I did, when I was a little girl and we used to work in wool from samplers, and learn to do alphabets. I'm glad you appreciate it. If you would like to have me embroider anything for the church, don't hesitate to ask me." She busied herself examining the stoles again, and asked:

"How much did these things cost, if you don't mind my askin'?"

"I don't know. They were given to me by a friend of mine, when I graduated from the Seminary."

"Hm! a friend of yours, eh? She must think an awful lot of you."

Hepsey gave Donald a sharp glance.

"I didn't say it was a lady."

"No, but your eyes and cheeks did. Well, it's none of my business, and there's no reason that I know of why the Devil should have all the bright colors, and embroideries, and things. Are you High Church?"

Maxwell hesitated a moment and replied:

"What do you mean by 'High Church?'"

"The last rector we had was awful high." Hepsey smiled with reminiscent amusement.

"How so?"

"We suspected he didn't wear no pants durin' service."

"How very extraordinary! Is that a symptom of ritualism?"

"Well, you see he wore a cassock under his surplice, and none of our parsons had ever done that before. The Senior Warden got real stirred up about it, and told Mr. Whittimore that our rectors always wore pants durin' service. Mr. Whittimore pulled up his cassock and showed the Warden that he had his pants on. The Warden told him it was an awful relief to his mind, as he considered goin' without pants durin' service the enterin' wedge for Popish tricks; and if things went on like that, nobody knew where we would land. Then some of the women got talkin', and said that the rector practiced celibacy, and that some one should warn him that the parish wouldn't stand for any more innovations, and he'd better look out. So one day, Virginia Bascom, the Senior Warden's daughter, told him what was being said about him. The parson just laughed at Ginty, and said that celibacy was his misfortune, not his fault; and that he hoped to overcome it in time. That puzzled her some, and she came to me and asked what celibacy was. When I told her it was staying unmarried, like St. Paul—my, but wasn't she mad, though! You ought to have seen her face. She was so mortified that she wouldn't speak to me for a week. Well, I guess I've gossiped enough for now. I must go and make my biscuits for supper. If I can help you any, just call out."

CHAPTER III
THE SENIOR WARDEN

"It's a fine morning, Mr. Maxwell," Mrs. Burke remarked at breakfast next day, "and I'm goin' to drive down to the village to do some shopping. Don't you want to go with me and pay your respects to the Senior Warden? You'll find him in his office. Then I'll meet you later, and bring you home—dead or alive!"

Maxwell laughed. "That sounds cheerful, but I should be glad to go."

"I guess you better, and have it over with. He'll expect it. He's like royalty: he never calls first; and when he's at home he always has a flag on a pole in the front yard. If he's out of town for the day, his man lowers the flag. I generally call when the flag's down. I wish everybody had a flag; it's mighty convenient."

The center of Durford's social, commercial and ecclesiastical life was the village green, a plot of ground on which the boys played ball, and in the middle of which was the liberty pole and the band-stand. On one side of the green was a long block of stores, and on the opposite side a row of churches, side by side, five in number. There was the Meeting House, in plain gray; "The First Church of Durford," with a Greek portico in front; "The Central Church," with a box-like tower and a slender steeple with a gilded rooster perched on top—an edifice which looked like a cross between a skating rink and a railroad station; and last of all, the Episcopal Church on the corner—a small, elongated structure, which might have been a carpenter-shop but for the little cross which surmounted the front gable, and the pointed tops of the narrow windows, which were supposed to be "gothic" and to proclaim the structure to be the House of God.

Just around the corner was a little tumble-down house known as "The Rectory." The tall grass and the lowered shades indicated that it had been unoccupied for some time. Mrs. Burke called Maxwell's attention to it.

"I suppose you'll be living there some day—if you stay here long enough; though of course you can't keep house there alone. The place needs a lot of over-haulin'. Nickey says there's six feet of plaster off the parlor ceilin', and the cellar gets full of water when it rains; but I guess we can fix it up when the time comes. That's your cathedral, on the corner. You see, we have five churches, when we really need only one; and so we have to scrap for each other's converts, to keep up the interest. We feed 'em on sandwiches, pickles and coffee every now and then, to make 'em come to church. Yes, preachin' and pickles, sandwiches and salvation, seem to run in the same class, these days."

When they arrived in front of the block, Mrs. Burke hitched her horse, and left Maxwell to his own devices. He proceeded to hunt up the post office; and as the mail was not yet distributed, he had to wait some time, conscious of the fact that he was the center of interest to the crowd assembled in the room. Finally, when he gained access to the delivery window, he was greeted by a smile from the postmistress, a woman of uncertain age, who remarked as she handed him his letters:

"Good morning, Mr. Maxwell. Glad to meet you. I'm a Presbyterian myself; but I have always made it a point to be nice to everybody. You seem to have quite a good many correspondents, and I presume you'll be wantin' a lock box. It's so convenient. You must feel lonesome in a strange place. Drop in and see mother some day. She's got curvature of the spine, but no religious prejudices. She'll be right glad to see you, I'm sure, even though she's not 'Piscopal."

Maxwell thanked her, and inquired the way to the Senior Warden's office, to which she directed him.

Three doors below the post office was a hallway and a flight of stairs leading up to Mr. Bascom's sanctum. As he ascended, Maxwell bethought him of the Bishop's hint that this was the main stronghold for the exercise of his strategy. The Senior Warden, for some reason or other, had persistently quarreled with the clergy, or crossed them. What was the secret of his antagonism? Would he be predisposed in Maxwell's favor, or prejudiced against him? He would soon discover—and he decided to let Bascom do most of the talking. Reaching the first landing, Donald knocked on a door the upper panel of which was filled with glass, painted white. On the glass in large black letters was the name: "SYLVESTER BASCOM."

The Senior Warden sat behind a table, covered with musty books and a litter of letters and papers. In his prime he had been a small man; and now, well past middle age, he looked as if he had shrunk until he was at least five sizes too small for his skin, which was sallow and loose. There was a suspicious look in his deep-set eyes, which made his hooked nose all the more aggressive. He was bald, except for a few stray locks of gray hair which were brushed up from his ears over the top of his head, and evidently fastened down by some gluey cosmetic. He frowned severely as Maxwell entered, but extended a shriveled, bony hand, and pointed to a chair. Then placing the tips of his fingers together in front of his chest, he gazed at Donald as if he were the prisoner at the bar, and began without any preliminary welcome:

"So you are the young man who is to take charge of the church. It is always difficult for a city-bred man to adjust himself to the needs and manners of a country parish. Very difficult, Mr. Maxwell—very difficult."

Maxwell smiled as he replied:

"Yes, but that is a fault which time will remedy."

"Doubtless. Time has a way of remedying most things. But in the meantime—in the meantime, lack of tact, self-assertiveness, indiscretion, on the part of a clergyman may do much harm—much harm!"

Mr. Maxwell colored slightly as he laughed and replied:

"I should imagine that you have had rather a 'mean time,' from the way you speak. Your impressions of the clergy seem to be painful."

"Well," the lawyer continued sententiously, "we have had all sorts and conditions of men, as the Prayer Book says; and the result has not *always* been satisfactory—*not* always satisfactory. But I was not consulted."

To this, Maxwell, who was somewhat nettled, replied:

"I suppose that in any case the responsibility for the success of a parish must be somewhat divided between the parson and the people. I am sure I may count on your assistance."

"Oh yes; oh yes; of course. I shall be very glad to advise you in any way I can. Prevention is better than cure: don't hesitate to come to me for suggestions. You will doubtless be anxious to follow in the good old ways, and avoid extremes. I am a firm believer in expediency. Though I was not consulted in the present appointment, I may say that what we need is a man of moderate views who can adjust himself to circumstances. Tact, that is the great thing in life. I am a firm believer in tact. Our resources are limited; and a clergyman should be a self-denying man of God, contented with plain living and high thinking. No man can succeed in a country parish who seeks the loaves and fishes of the worldling. Durford is not a metropolis; we do not emulate city ways."

"No, I should imagine not," Maxwell answered.

The parson gathered that the Senior Warden felt slighted that he had not been asked by the Bishop to name his appointee; and that if he had bethought himself to sprinkle a little hay-seed on his clothing, his reception might have been more cordial.

At this point the door opened and a woman, hovering somewhere between twenty-five and forty, dressed in rather youthful and pronounced attire, entered, and seeing Donald exclaimed:

"Oh, papa, I did not know that you were busy with a client. Do excuse me."

Then, observing the clerical attire of the "client," she came forward, and extending her hand to Donald, exclaimed with a coy, insinuating smile:

"I am sure that you must be Mr. Maxwell. I am so glad to see you. I hope I am not interrupting professional confidences."

"Not in the least," Donald replied, as he placed a chair for her. "I am very glad to have the pleasure of meeting you, Miss Bascom."

"I heard last night that you had arrived, Mr. Maxwell; and I am sure that it is very good of you to come and see papa so soon. I hope to see you at our house before long. You know that we are in the habit of seeing a good deal of the rector, because—you will excuse my frankness—because there are so few people of culture and refinement in this town to make it pleasant for him."

"I am sure that you are very kind," Donald replied. Miss Bascom had adjusted her tortoise-shell lorgnette, and was surveying Donald from head to foot.

"Is your wife with you?" she inquired, as one who would say: "Tell me no lies!"

"No, I am not married."

At once she was one radiant smile of welcome:

"Papa, we must do all we can to make Mr. Maxwell feel at home at Willow Bluff—so that he will not get lonesome and desert us," she added genially.

"You're very kind."

"You must come and dine with us very soon and see our place for yourself. You are staying with Mrs. Burke, I understand."

"Yes."

"How does she impress you?"

"I hardly know her well enough to form any definite opinion of her, though she has been kindness itself to me."

"Yes, she has a sharp tongue, but a kind heart; and she does a great deal of good in the village; but, poor soul! she has no sense of humor—none whatever. Then of course she is not in society, you know. You will find, Mr. Maxwell, that social lines are very carefully drawn in this town; there are so many grades, and one has to be careful, you know."

"Is it so! How many people are there in the town?"

"Possibly eight or nine hundred."

"And how many of them are 'in society'?"

"Oh, I should imagine not more than twenty or thirty."

"They must be very select."

"Oh, we are; quite so."

"Don't you ever get tired of seeing the same twenty or thirty all the time? I'm afraid I am sufficiently vulgar to like a change, once in a while—somebody real common, you know."

Miss Bascom raised her lorgnette in pained surprise and gazed at Donald curiously; then she sighed and tapping her fingers with her glasses replied:

"But one has to consider the social responsibilities of one's position, you know. Many of the village people are well enough in their way, really quite amusing as individuals; but one cannot alter social distinctions."

"I see," replied Donald, non-committally.

Virginia was beginning to think that the new rector was rather dull in his perceptions, rather *gauche*, but, deciding to take a charitable view, she held out her hand with a beaming smile as she said:

"Remember, you are to make Willow Bluff one of your homes. We shall always be charmed to see you."

When, after their respective shoppings were completed, Maxwell rejoined Mrs. Burke, and they had started on a brisk trot towards home, she remarked:

"So you have had a visit with the Senior Warden."

"Yes, and with Miss Bascom. She came into the office while I was there."

"Hm! Well! She's one of your flock!"

"Would you call Miss Bascom one of my lambs?" asked Donald mischievously.

"Oh, that depends on where you draw the line. Don't you think she's handsome?"

"I can hardly say. What do you think about it?"

"Oh, I don't know. When she's well dressed she has a sort of style about her; but isn't it merciful that we none of us know how we really do look? If we did, we wouldn't risk bein' alone with ourselves five minutes without a gun."

"Is that one for Miss Bascom?"

"No, I ought not to say a word against Virginia Bascom. She's a good sort accordin' to her lights; and then too, she is a disconnection of mine by marriage—once removed."

"How do you calculate that relationship?"

"Oh, her mother's brother married my sister. She suspected that he was guilty of incompatibility—and she proved it, and got a divorce. If that don't make a disconnection of Ginty Bascom, then I don't know what does. Virginia was born in Boston, though she was brought up here. It must be terrible to be born in Boston, and have to live up to it, when you spend your whole life in a place like Durford. But Ginty does her very best, though occasionally she forgets."

"You can hardly blame her for that. Memory is tricky, and Boston and Durford are about as unlike as two places well could be."

"Oh, no; I don't blame her. Once she formed a club for woman's suffrage. She set out to 'form my mind'—as if my mind wasn't pretty thoroughly formed at this time of day—and get me to protest against the tyranny of the male sex. I didn't see that the male sex was troublin' her much; but I signed a petition she got up to send to the Governor or somebody, asking for the right to vote. There was an opposition society that didn't want the ballot, and they got up another petition."

"And you signed that too, I expect," laughed Donald.

"Sure thing, I did. I'm not narrow-minded, and I like to be obliging. Then she tried what she called slummin', which, as near as I can see, means walkin' in where you 'aint wanted, because people are poorer than you are, and leavin' little tracts that nobody reads, and currant jelly that nobody eats, and clothes that nobody can wear. But an Irishman shied a cabbage at her head while she was tryin' to convince him that the bath-tub wasn't really a coal bin, and that his mental attitude was hindside before.

"Then she got to be a Theosophist, and used to sit in her room upstairs projecting her astral body out of the window into the back yard, and pulling it in again like a ball on a rubber string—just for practice, you know. But that attack didn't last long."

"She seems to be a very versatile young woman; but she doesn't stick to one thing very long."

"A rolling stone gathers no moss, you know," Mrs. Burke replied. "That's one of the advantages of bein' a rolling stone. It must be awful to get mossy; and there isn't any moss on Virginia Bascom, whatever faults she may have—not a moss."

For a moment Mrs. Burke was silent, and then she began:

"Once Virginia got to climbin' her family tree, to find out where her ancestors came from. She thought that possibly they might be noblemen. But I guess there wasn't very much doin' up the tree until she got down to New York, and paid a man to tell her. She brought back an illuminated coat of arms with a lion rampantin' on top; but she was the same old Virginia still. What do I care about my ancestors! It doesn't make no difference to me. I'm just myself anyway, no matter how you figure; and I'm a lot more worried about where I'm goin' to, than where I came from. Virginia's got a book called 'Who's Who,' that she's always studying. But the only thing that matters, it seems to me, is Who's What."

"I wonder she hasn't married," remarked Donald, innocently.

"Ah, that's the trouble. She's like a thousand others without no special occupation in life. She's wastin' a lot of bottled up interest and sympathy on foolish things. If she'd married and had seven babies, they would have seen to it that she didn't make a fool of herself. However, it isn't her fault. She's volunteered to act as Deaconess to every unmarried parson we've had; and it's a miracle of wonders one of 'em didn't succumb; parsons are such—oh, do excuse me! I mean so injudicious on the subject of matrimony."

"But, Mrs. Burke, don't you think a clergyman ought to be a married man?"

"Well, to tell you the truth, t'aint me that's been doin' the thinkin' along those lines, for most of the parsons we've had. I've been more of a first aid to the injured, in the matrimonial troubles of our parish, and the Lord only knows when love-making has got as far as actual injury to the parties engaged,—well thinkin' 'aint much use. But there's Ginty for example. She's been worryin' herself thin for the last five years, doin' matrimonial equations for the clergy. She's a firm believer in the virtue of patience, and if the Lord only keeps on sendin' us unmarried rectors, Ginty is goin' to have her day. It's just naturally bound to come. I 'aint sure whether she's got a right to be still runnin' with the lambs or not, but that don't matter much,—old maids will rush in where angels fear to tread."

Maxwell smiled. "Old maids, and old bachelors, are pretty much alike. I know a few of the latter, that no woman on earth could make into regular human beings."

"Oh, yes; old bachelors aren't the nicest thing the Lord ever made. Most of 'em are mighty selfish critters, take 'em as they run; and a man that's never had a real great love in his life doesn't know what life is."

"That's quite true," Donald responded, with such warmth that Mrs. Burke glanced at him suspiciously, and changed her tune, as she continued:

"Seems to me a parson, or any other man, is very foolish to marry before he can support a wife comfortably, and lay by somethin' for a rainy day, though. The last rector had five babies and seventeen cents to feed 'em with. Yes, there were little olive branches on all four sides of the table, and under the table too. The Whittimores seemed to have their quiver full of 'em, as the psalmist says. Mrs. Whittimore used to say to me, 'The Lord will provide,'—just to keep her courage up, poor thing! Well, I suppose the Lord did provide; but I had to do a lot of hustlin', just the same. No sir, if a parson marries, he better find a woman who has outgrown her short skirts. Young things dyin' to be martyrs with a good lookin' young parson, are a drug in the market. Better go slow." And Hepsey looked up at him significantly.

"Then you think it would be inadvisable to propose to Miss Virginia immediately, do you?" Donald asked, as if humbly seeking guidance.

"Well, there doesn't seem to be any immediate hurry about it. Now if you'll open the gate to Thunder Cliff, I'll be much obliged to you. If I don't get my mind on something less romantic than Virginia, we shall have to dine off airy fancies—and that won't suit Nickey, for one."

CHAPTER IV
MILKING

Betty, my love:

I can imagine that just about this time you have finished your dinner, and are enjoying your after-dinner coffee in the library with your father. I would give all that I possess, though heaven knows that is mighty little, to be with you and get you to talk to me, and let me tell you all that has happened since I left you. But instead of that I am alone in my room with your picture on the table while I write, and it is the middle of the evening with us on the farm. I have a bright wood fire on the hearth, as it's a bit chilly to-night.

To-day I have almost completed my first round of parish visits, and the experience has been a revelation to me of the mixture of pathetic narrowness, hardship, and self-denial of the people up here in the mountains. One minute I am all out of patience with their stupidity, and the next I am touched to the heart by their patience with unendurable conditions, and their generosity and kindness to each other. I hope to be able to adjust my mental equilibrium to the situation before long and to learn to understand them better; I find that a country parson must be a man of many accomplishments, and that I have to learn my profession all over again. Yesterday I called on a poor shriveled old woman who, I was told, was in trouble. When I asked her what I could do for her, she brightened up and informed me that her apple trees were full of worms! So there was nothing for it but to take off my coat and vest, roll up my sleeves, and burn out the worms. I must have destroyed about a bushel, more or less. It took most of the afternoon; but she was pleased, and appeared in church this morning for the first time in six years.

I have learned a lot about the rotation of crops, helped to dig a well, and attended a barn dance. I have eaten pickles by the score at teas given in my honor, rather than offend the hostess; and have had horrible nights in consequence. Every morning Nickey and I take the milk down to the creamery before breakfast. I am so tanned that you would hardly recognize me; and I must confess with shame that I am never more happy than when I am able to put on my soiled working clothes and do manual labor on the farm. I suppose it is the contrast to my former life, and the fact that it takes my thoughts away from the longing for you.

The men up here seem to think I know mighty little. It's very humiliating! But since they discovered that I am neither "'ristocratic" nor "pious," they seem to be friendly enough. I often find myself wondering if much of the work in the seminary wasn't a sheer waste of time, when I am brought up against the practical, commonplace, everyday life of these people. My friend Mrs. Burke has a fund of common sense and worldly wisdom which is worth more than any Ph.D. or S.T.D. represents, to help a man to meet the hard facts of life successfully; and she has been very nice and considerate in making suggestions to me—always wrapped up in a humor all her own. I have found it practically impossible to get into touch with the farmers of the neighborhood without becoming more or less of a farmer myself, and learning by actual experience what the life is like. One man was so openly supercilious when he found out that I did not know how to milk, that Mrs. Burke, who is nothing if not practical, offered to show me.

I have acquired a suit of overalls, and a wide-brimmed straw hat; and so, attiring myself in the most orthodox fashion, Mrs. Burke and I went to the shed yesterday where Louise, the Jersey cow, abides, and I took my first lesson in milking. Mrs. Burke carefully explained to me the *modus operandi* I was to pursue; and so, taking the tin pail between my knees, I seated myself on the three-legged stool by the side of Louise, and timidly began operations. She seemed to know by some bovine instinct that I was a tenderfoot; and although I followed Mrs. Burke's instructions to the letter, no milk put in its appearance. Mrs. Burke was highly amused at my perplexity. Finally she remarked:

"You've got to introduce yourself, and get Louise's confidence before she'll give down. She thinks that you are too familiar on a short acquaintance. Now talk to her a bit, and be friendly."

This was somewhat of a poser, as Louise and I really have not much in common, and I was at a loss where to begin. But something had to be done, and so I made a venture and remarked:

"Louise, the wind is in the south; and if it doesn't change, we shall certainly have rain within three days."

This did not seem to have the desired effect. In fact, she ignored my remark in the most contemptuous fashion. Then Mrs. Burke suggested:

"Get up, and come round where she can see you. No lady wants to be talked to by a gentleman that's out of sight."

So I got up and went around by her head, fed her some clover, patted her on the neck, rubbed her nose, and began a little mild, persuasive appeal:

"Louise, I am really a man of irreproachable character. I am a son of the Revolution; I held three scholarships in Harvard; and I graduated second in my class at the General Sem. Furthermore, I'm not at all accustomed to being snubbed by ladies. Can't you make up your mind to be obliging?"

Louise sniffed at me inquiringly, gazing at me with large-eyed curiosity. Then as if in token that she had come to a favorable conclusion, she ran out her tongue and licked my hand. When I resumed operations, the milk poured into the pail, and Mrs. Burke was just congratulating me on my complete success, when, by some accident the stool slipped, and I fell over backwards, and the whole contents of the pail was poured on the ground. My! but wasn't I disgusted? I thought Mrs. Burke would never stop laughing at me; but she was good enough not to allude to the loss of the milk!

Some day when we are married, and you come up here, I will take you out and introduce you to Louise, and she will fall in love with you on the spot.

My most difficult task is my Senior Warden—and it looks as if he *would not* make friends, do what I will to "qualify" according to his own expressed notions of what a country parson should be. But I rather suspect that he likes to keep the scepter in his own hands, while the clergy do his bidding. But that won't do for me.

So you see the life up here is interesting from its very novelty, though I do get horribly lonesome, sometimes. If I had not pledged myself to the Bishop to stay and work the parish together into something like an organization, I am afraid I should be tempted to cut and run—back to you, sweetheart.

And there was a post script:

"I've not said half enough of how much Mrs. Burke's wisdom has taught and helped me. She is a shrewd observer of human motives, and I expect she has had a struggle to keep the sweetness of her nature at the top. She is, naturally, a capable, dominating character; and often I watch how she forces herself to let persuasiveness take precedence of combativeness. Her acquired philosophy, as applied to herself and others, is summed up in a saying she let drop the other day, modified to suit her needs: 'More flies are caught with molasses than with vinegar—but keep some vinegar by you!' *Verb. Sap.!*"

CHAPTER V
THE MINIATURE

It happened that the Reverend Donald Maxwell committed a careless indiscretion. When he went to his room to prepare for supper, he found that he had left the miniature of a certain young lady on the mantelpiece, having forgotten to return it to its hiding-place the night before. He quickly placed it in its covering and locked it up in his desk, but not without many misgivings at the thought that Mrs. Burke had probably discovered it when she put his room in order.

He was quite right in his surmise, for just as she was about to leave the room she had caught sight of the picture, and, after examining it carefully, she had exclaimed to herself:

"Hm! Hm! So that's the young woman, is it? In a gilded frame set with real glass rubies and turquoises. I guessed those letters couldn't come from his mother. She wouldn't write to him every blessed day; she'd take a day off now and then, just to rest up a bit. Well, well, well! So this is what you've been dreaming about; and a mighty good thing too—only the sooner it's known the better. But I suppose I'll have to wait for his reverence to inform me officially, and then I'll have to look mighty surprised! She's got a good face, anyway; but he ought to wait awhile. Poor soul! she'd just die of loneliness up here. Well, I suppose it'll be my business to look after her, and I reckon I'd best take time by the fetlock, and get the rectory in order. It isn't fit for rats to live in now."

Mrs. Burke's discovery haunted her all day long, and absorbed her thoughts when she went to bed. If Maxwell was really engaged to be married, she did not see why he did not announce the fact, and have it over with. She had to repeat her prayers three times before she could keep the girl in the gilt frame out of them; and she solved the problem by praying that she might not make a fool of herself.

The next morning she went over to Jonathan Jackson's house to see what her friend and neighbor, the Junior Warden, would say about the matter. He could be trusted to keep silent and assist her to carry out some provisional plans. She knew exactly what she wished and what she intended to do; but she imagined that she wanted the pleasure of hearing some one tell her that she was exactly right.

Jonathan Jackson was precisely the person to satisfy the demand, as his deceased wife had never allowed him to have any opinion for more than fifteen minutes at a time—if it differed from hers; and when she had made a pretense of consulting him, he had learned by long experience to hesitate for a moment, look judicially wise, and then repeat her suggestions as nearly as he could remember them. So Jonathan made a most excellent friend and neighbor, when any crisis or emergency called for an expert opinion.

Mrs. Burke had been an intimate friend of Sarah Jackson, and just before Mrs. Jackson died she made Hepsey promise that after she was gone she would keep a friendly eye on Jonathan, and see that he did not get into mischief, or let the house run down, or "live just by eatin' odds and ends off the pantry shelf any old way." Mrs. Jackson entertained no illusions in regard to her husband, and she trusted Hepsey implicitly. So, after Mrs. Jackson's mortal departure, Hepsey made periodic calls on Jonathan, which always gave him much pleasure until she became inquisitive about his methods of housekeeping; then he would grow reticent.

"Good morning, Jonathan," Hepsey called, as she presented herself at the woodshed door, where she caught Jonathan mending some of his underclothes laboriously.

"Well, I declare," she continued, "I'm blessed if you 'aint sewin' white buttons on with black thread. Is anybody dead in the family, or 'aint you feelin' well as to your head this mornin'?"

His voice quavered with mingled embarrassment and resentment as he replied:

"What difference does it make, Hepsey? It don't make no difference, as long as nobody don't see it but me."

"And why in the name of conscience don't you get a thimble, Jonathan? The idea of your stickin' the needle in, and then pressin' it against the chair to make it go through. If that 'aint just like a helpless man, I wouldn't say."

"Well, of course sewin' 'aint just a man's business, anyway; and when he has just got to do it—"

"Why don't you let Mary McGuire do it for you? You pay her enough, certainly, to keep you from becomin' a buttonless orphan."

Mary McGuire, be it said, was the woman who came in by the day, and cooked for Jonathan, and intermittently cleaned him out of house and home.

"She don't know much about such things," replied Jonathan confidentially. "I did let her do it for a while; but when my buttonholes got tore larger, instead of sewin' 'em up, she just put on a larger button; and I'd be buttonin' my pants with the covers of saucepans by now, if I'd let her go on."

"It is curious what helpless critters men are, specially widowers. Now Jonathan, why don't you lay aside your sewin', and invite me into your parlor? You aren't a bit polite."

"Well, come along then, Hepsey; but the parlor aint just in apple-pie order, as you might say. Things are mussed up a bit." He looked at her suspiciously.

"I'M BLESSED IF YOU 'AINT SEWIN' WHITE BUTTONS ON
WITH BLACK THREAD. IS ANYBODY DEAD IN THE FAMILY,
OR 'AINT YOU FEELIN' WELL THIS MORNIN'?"

When they entered the parlor Mrs. Burke gazed about in a critical
sort of way.

"Jonathan Jackson, if you don't get married again before long I don't
know what'll become of you," she remarked, as she wrote her name
with the end of her finger in the dust on the center-table. "Why
don't you open the parlor occasionally and let the air in? It smells
that musty in here I feel as if I was attendin' your wife's funeral all
over again."

"Well, of course you know we never did use the parlor much, 'cept there was a funeral in the family, or you called, or things like that."

"Thank *you*; but even so, you might put things away occasionally, and not leave them scattered all over the place."

"What's the use? I never can find anything when it's where it belongs; but if it's left just where I drop it, I know right where it is when I want it."

"That's a man's argument. Sakes alive! The least you could do would be to shut your bureau drawers."

"What's the use shuttin' bureau drawers when you've got to open 'em again 'fore long?" Jonathan asked. "It just makes so much more trouble; and there's trouble enough in this world, anyway."

"You wouldn't dare let things go like this when Sarah was livin'."

"No," Jonathan replied sadly, "but there's some advantages in bein' a widower. Of course I don't mean no disrespect to Sarah, but opinions will differ about some things. She'd never let me go up the front stairs without takin' my boots off, so as not to soil the carpet; and when she died and the relatives tramped up and down reckless like, I almost felt as if it was wicked. For a fact, I did."

"Well, I always told Sarah she was a slave to dust; I believe that dust worried her a lot more than her conscience, poor soul. I should think that Mary McGuire would tidy up for you a little bit once in a while."

"Well, Mary does the best she knows how. But I like her goin' better than comin'. The fact is, a man of my age can't live alone always, Hepsey. It's a change to live this way, till—"

"Oh, heaven save the mark! I can't stay here talkin' all day; but I'll tidy up a bit before I go, if you don't mind, Jonathan. You go on with what you call your sewin'."

"Go ahead, Hepsey. You can do anything you like," he replied, beaming upon her.

Mrs. Burke opened the blinds and windows, shook up the pillows on the lounge, straightened the furniture, dusted off the chairs and opened the door to the porch. She made a flying trip to the garden, and returned with a big bunch of flowers which she placed in a large glass vase on the mantel. Then she hung Jonathan's dressing gown over the back of a chair, and put his slippers suggestively near at hand. In a few moments she had transformed the whole appearance of the room, giving it a look of homelike coziness which had long been foreign to it.

"There now, Jonathan! That's better, isn't it?"

Jonathan sighed profoundly as he replied:

"It certainly is, Hepsey; it certainly is. I wonder why a man can't do that kind of thing like a woman can? He knows somethin's wrong, but he can't tell what it is."

Hepsey had almost forgotten her errand; but now that her work was done it came back to her with sudden force; so, puckering up her lips and scowling severely at the carpet, she began:

"The fact is, Jonathan, I didn't come over here to dust the parlor or to jolly you. I've come to have a confidential talk with you about a matter of great importance."

"What is it, Hepsey?"

"Matrimony."

Jonathan started eagerly, and colored with self-conscious embarrassment; and after clearing his throat, nervously inquired:

"Did you think of contemplatin' matrimony again, Hepsey?— though this 'aint leap year."

"I, contemplate matrimony? Oh, land of Gideon, *no*. It's about some one else. Don't get scared. I'm no kidnapper!"

"Well, who is it, then?" Jonathan inquired, with a touch of disappointment.

"My adopted son."

"You don't say! I've heard rumors about Maxwell and Virginia Bascom; but I didn't take no stock in 'em, knowin' Virginia."

"Virginia hasn't nothin' to do with it."

"Well, who has then, for land's sake!"

"I don't know the girl's name; but I saw her picture on his mantelpiece yesterday mornin', and I've had my suspicions for some time."

"Well, I suppose his marryin' 'aint none of our business anyway, be it?"

"Yes, it is our business; if he's goin' to get married, the rectory's got to be fixed over a whole lot 'fore it's fit to live in. You know the Senior Warden won't lift his finger, and you've got to help me do it."

Jonathan sighed profoundly, knowing from past experience that Hepsey's word carried more weight than all the vestry.

"I suppose I have, if you say so, Hepsey."

"Yes sir, you've got to help me do it. No decent girl is goin' into that house as it is, with my consent. It's the worst old rat-trap I ever saw. I've got the key, and I'm goin' through it this afternoon, and then I'm goin' to plan what ought to be done."

"But it seems to me you're venturin' some. You don't *know* they're goin' to be married."

"No, but all the symptoms point that way, and we've got to be prepared for it."

"But the people round town seem to think that Virginia has a first mortgage on the rector already."

"No doubt *she* thinks she has; but it 'aint true. He's made a blunder, though, not announcin' his engagement, and I'm goin' to tell him so the first chance I get. I don't see why he should air his private affairs all over the town, but if he don't announce his engagement before long, Virginia Bascom'll make an awful row when he does."

"Yes, and to the best of my knowledge and belief this'll be her fifth row."

"Well, you meet me at the rectory at two o'clock sharp."

"But we ought to consult the vestry first," the Junior Warden cautioned her.

"What for, I'd like to know?"

"'Cause they are the trustees of the property."

"Then why don't they 'tend to the property? The vestry are a lot of–"

"Sh! Hepsey, be careful. I'll be there, I'll be there!"

Mrs. Burke rose and started for the door; but Jonathan called out to her:

"Hepsey, can't you stay to dinner? I'd like awful well to have you. It would seem so nice and homelike to see you sittin' opposite me at the table."

"Am I to consider this a proposal of marriage, Jonathan?"

"Well, I hadn't thought of it in that light; but if *you* would, I'd be mighty thankful."

But Hepsey was beating her retreat.

Jonathan stood for a minute or two in the middle of the room and looked very sober. Slowly he took off his coat and put on his dressing gown. Then he sat down, and cautiously put his feet in another chair. Next he lighted a cigar—gazing about the room as if his late wife might appear at any moment as an avenging deity, and drag him into the kitchen where he belonged. But nothing happened, and he began to feel a realization of his independence. He sat and thought for a long time, and a mighty hunger of the heart overwhelmed him. Before he knew it, a tear or two had fallen on the immaculate carpet; and then, suddenly recollecting himself, he stood up, saying to himself—such is the consistency of man:

"Sarah was a good soul accordin' to her lights; but she's dead, and I must confess I'm powerful reconciled. Hepsey Burke's different. I wonder if—"

But he put he thought away from him with a "get thee behind me" abruptness, and putting on his coat, went out to water the stock.

CHAPTER VI
THE MISSIONARY TEA

"Hm!" Mrs. Burke remarked to Maxwell abruptly one day during supper. "We haven't had a missionary tea since you came, and I think it's high time we did."

"What sort of a missionary tea do you mean?" the parson inquired.

"Well," Mrs. Burke responded, "our missionary teas combine different attractions. We get together and look over each other's clothes; that's the first thing; then some one reads a paper reportin' how things is goin' in Zanzibar, or what's doin' in Timbuctoo. Then we look over the old clothes sent in for missionaries, mend 'em up, and get 'em ready to send off. Then we have tea and cake. I've had my misgivin' for some time that perhaps we cared more for the tea and cake than we did for the heathen; but of course I put such a wicked thought aside. If you value your reputation for piety, don't you ever speak of a missionary tea here except in a whisper."

"But I suppose the tea helps to get people together and be more sociable?"

"Certainly. The next best thing to religion is a cup of strong tea and a frosted cake, to make us country people friends. Both combined can't be beat. But you ought to see the things that have been sent in this last week for the missionary box. There's a smoking jacket, two pairs of golf-trousers, several pairs of mismated gloves, a wonderful lot of undarned stockings, bonnets and underclothes to burn, two jackets and a bathin' suit. I wonder what people think missionaries are doin' most of the time!"

On the day appointed for the missionary tea the ladies were to assemble at Thunder Cliff at four o'clock; and when Maxwell came home, before the advent of the first guest, he seemed somewhat depressed; and Mrs. Burke inquired:

"Been makin' calls on your parishioners?"

"Yes, I have made a few visits."

"Now you must look more cheerful, or somebody'll suspect that you don't always find parish calls the joy of your life."

"It's so difficult to find subjects of conversation that they are interested in. I simply couldn't draw out Mrs. Snodgrass, for instance."

"Well, when you've lived in the country as long as I have, you'll find that the one unfailin' subject of interest is symptoms—mostly dyspepsy and liver complaint. If you had known enough to have started right with Elmira Snodgrass, she would have thawed out at once. Elmira is always lookin' for trouble as the sparks fly upwards, or thereabouts. She'd crawl through a barbed wire fence if she couldn't get at it any other way. She always chews a pill on principle, and then she calls it a dispensation of Providence, and wonders why she was ever born to be tormented."

"In that case," laughed Maxwell, "I'd better get some medical books and read up on symptoms. By the by, is there any particular program for this missionary meeting, Mrs. Burke?"

"Yes, Virginia Bascom's goin' to read a paper called 'The Christian Mother as a Missionary in her own Household.' To be sure, Ginty's no Christian Mother, or any other kind of a mother; but she's as full of enthusiasm as a shad is of bones. She'd bring up any child while you wait, and not charge a cent. There goes the bell, so please excuse me."

The guests were received by Mrs. Burke. Miss Bascom entered the parlor with a portentous bundle of manuscript under her arm, and greeted Donald with a radiant smile. Pulling a pansy from a bunch in her dress, she adjusted it in his buttonhole with the happy shyness of a young kitten chasing its tail. After the others had assembled, they formed a circle to inspect the clothing which had been sent in. There was a general buzz of conversation.

As they were busily going through the garments, Virginia remarked, "Are all these things to go to the missionaries at Tien Tsin?" and she adjusted her lorgnette to inspect the heap.

"Yes," Mrs. Burke responded wearily, "and I hope they'll get what comfort they can out of 'em."

"You don't seem to be very appreciative, Mrs. Burke," Virginia reproved.

"Well, I suppose I ought to be satisfied," Hepsey replied. "But it does seem as if most people give to the Lord what they can't use for themselves any longer—as they would to a poor relation that's worthy, but not to be coddled by too much charity."

"I think these things are quite nice enough for the missionaries," Virginia retorted. "They are thankful for anything."

"Yes, I know," Mrs. Burke replied calmly. "Missionaries and their families have no business to have any feelings that can't be satisfied with second-hand clothes, and no end of good advice on how to spend five cents freely but not extravagantly."

"But don't you believe in sending them useful things?" Virginia asked loftily.

"So I do; but I'd hate that word 'useful' if I was a missionary's wife."

"Might I inquire," asked Miss Bascom meekly, "what you would send?"

"Certainly! I'd send a twenty-five-cent scent bag, made of silk and filled with patchouli-powder," said Hepsey, squarely.

"Well," Virginia added devoutly, "satchet bags may be well enough in their place; but they won't feed missionaries, or clothe them, or save souls, you know, Mrs. Burke."

"Did anybody say they would?" Mrs. Burke inquired. "I shouldn't particularly care to see missionaries clothed in sachet bags myself; the smell might drive the heathen to desperation. But do we always limit our spending money to necessary clothes and food? The truth is, we all of us spend anything we like as long as it goes on our backs, or down our throats; but the moment it comes to supportin' missionaries we think 'em worldly and graspin' if they show any ambition beyond second-hand clothes."

"Do you live up to your preachin', Mrs. Burke?" a little sallow-faced woman inquired from a dark corner of the room.

"Oh, no; it hits me just as hard as anybody else, as Martin Luther said. But I've got a proposition to make: if you'll take these things you brought, back with you, and wear 'em for a week just as they are, and play you're the missionaries, I'll take back all I've said."

As, however, there was no response to this challenge, the box was packed, and the cover nailed down.

(It is perhaps no proper part of this story to add, that its opening on the other side of the world was attended by the welcome and surprising fragrance of patchouli, emanating from a little silk sachet secreted among the more workaday gifts.)

The ladies then adjourned to the front piazza, where the supper was served.

When the dishes had been cleared away, the guests adjusted their chairs and assumed attitudes of expectant attention while Virginia stood up and shyly unrolled her manuscript, with a placid, self-conscious smile on her countenance. She apologized for her youth and inexperience, with a moving glance towards her pastor, and then got down to business. She began with the original and striking remark that it was the chief glory and function of woman to be a home-maker. She continued with something to the effect that the woman who forms the character of her children in the sanctity of the home-life rules the destinies of the world. Then she made a fetching allusion to the "Mother of the Gracchi," and said something about jewels. Nobody knew who the "Gracchi" were, but they supposed that they must be some relatives of Virginia's who lived in Boston.

She asserted that the modern methods of bringing up children were all wrong. She drew a striking picture of the ideal home in which children always stood modestly and reverently by their parents' chairs, consumed with anxiety to be of some service to their elders. They were always to be immaculately neat in their attire, and gentle in their ways. The use of slang was quite beneath them.

These ideal children were always to spend their evenings at home in the perusal of instructive books, and the pursuit of useful knowledge. Then, when half-past seven arrived, they were to rise spontaneously and promptly, and bid their parents an affectionate good-night, and retire to their rooms, where, having said their prayers and recited the golden text, they were to get into bed.

Portions of Virginia's essay were quite moving. Speaking of the rewards which good mothers reap, in the virtues and graces of their dutiful offspring, she said:

"What mother does not feel a thrill of exquisite rapture as she fondly gazes into the depths of her baby's eyes and sees there the budding promise of glorious womanhood. What mother does not watch the development of her little son with wondering pride, as she notes his manly, simple ways, his gentle reverence, his tender, modest behavior. What mother—"

Here Virginia came to an abrupt stop, for there was a terrible racket somewhere overhead on the piazza roof; a rope was suddenly dropped over the edge of the eaves, and almost immediately a pair of very immodestly bare legs were lowered into view, followed by the rest of Nickey Burke's person, attired in his nightshirt. It was the work of a moment for the nimble boy to slide down the rope onto the ground. But, as he landed on his feet, finding himself in the august presence of the missionary circle, he remarked "Gee Whitaker bee's wax!" and prudently took to his heels, and sped around the house as if he had been shot out of a gun.

Several segments of the circle giggled violently. The essayist, though very red, made a brave effort to ignore the highly indecorous interruption, and so continued with trembling tones:

"What more beautiful and touching thing is there, than the innocent, unsullied modesty of childhood? One might almost say—"

But she never said it, for here again she was forced to pause while another pair of immodest legs appeared over the eaves, much fatter and shorter than the preceding pair. These belonged to Nickey's boon-companion, the gentle Oliver Wendell Jones. The rest of O. W. J. followed in due time; and, quite ignorant of what awaited him, he began his wriggling descent. Most unfortunately for him, the hem of his nightshirt caught on a large nail in the eaves of the roof; and after a frantic, fruitless, and fearful effort to disconnect himself, he hung suspended in the breeze for one awful moment, like a painted cherub on a Christmas tree, while his mother, recognizing her offspring, rose to go to his assistance.

Then there was a frantic yell, a terrible ripping sound, and Oliver Wendell was seen to drop to the ground clad in the sleeves and the front breadth of his shirt, while the entire back of it, from the collar down, waved triumphantly aloft from the eaves. Oliver Wendell Jones picked himself up, unhurt, but much frightened, and very angry: presenting much the aspect of a punctured tire. Then suddenly discovering the proximity of the missionary circle and missing the rear elevation of his shirt about the same time, in the horror and mortification of the moment, he lost his head entirely. Notwithstanding the protests of his pursuing mother, without waiting for his clothes, he fled, "anywhere, anywhere out of the world," bawling with wrath and chagrin.

The entire circumference of the missionary circle now burst into roars of laughter. His mother quickly overtook and captured Oliver, tying her apron around his neck as a concession to the popular prejudice against "the altogether." The gravity of the missionary circle was so thoroughly demoralized that it was impossible to restore order; and Miss Bascom, in the excess of her mortification, stuffed the rest of her manuscript, its eloquent peroration undelivered, into her bag.

"NICHOLAS BURKE, WHAT IN THE NAME OF CONSCIENCE
DOES ALL THIS IDIOTIC PERFORMANCE MEAN, I'D LIKE TO
KNOW?"

When the last guest had departed, Mrs. Burke proceeded to hunt up
Nickey, who was dressed and sitting on the top of the corn-crib
whittling a stick. His mother began:

"Nicholas Burke, what in the name of conscience does all this idiotic
performance mean, I'd like to know?"

Nickey closed his knife. Gazing serenely down at his mother, he
replied:

"How'd I know the blamed missionary push was goin' to meet on
the front porch, I'd like to know? Me and Oliver Wendell was just
playin' the house was on fire. We'd gone to bed in the front room,
and then I told Ollie the fire was breakin' out all around us, and the

sparks was flyin', and the stairs was burned away, and there was no way of 'scapin' but to slide down the rope over the roof. I 'aint to blame for his nightshirt bein' caught on a nail, and bein' ripped off him. Maybe the ladies was awful shocked; but they laughed fit to split their sides just the same. Mr. Maxwell laughed louder than 'em all."

Hepsey retired hastily, lest her face should relax its well-assumed severity.

Maxwell, in the meantime, felt it a part of his duty to console and soothe the ruffled feelings of his zealous and fluent parishioner, and to Virginia's pride his offer of escort to Willow Bluff was ample reparation for the untoward interruption of her oratory. She delivered into his hands, with sensitive upward glance, the receptacle containing her manuscript, and set a brisk pace, at which she insured the passing of the other guests along the road, making visible her triumph over circumstance and at the same time obviating untimely intrusion of a tete-a-tete conversation.

"You must have given a great deal of time and study to your subject," remarked Maxwell politely.

"It is very near to my heart," responded Virginia, in welling tones. "Home-life is, to me, almost a religion. Do you not feel, with me, that it is the most valuable of human qualities, Mr. Maxwell?"

"I do indeed, and one of the most difficult to reduce to a science," — she glanced up at him apprehensively, whereupon, lest he seemed to have erred in fact, he added, —"as you made us realize in your paper."

"It is so nice to have your appreciation," she gurgled. "Often I feel it almost futile to try to influence our cold parish audiences; their attitude is so stolid, so unimaginative. As you must have realized, in the pulpit, they are so hard to lead into untrodden paths. Let us take the way home by the lane," she added coyly, leading off the road down a sheltered by-way.

The lane was rough, and the lady, tightly and lightly shod, stumbled neatly and grasped her escort's arm for support—and retained it for comfort.

"What horizons your sermons have spread before us—and, yet,"—she hesitated,—"I often wonder, as my eyes wander over the congregation, how many besides myself, really hear your message, really see what *you* see."

Her hand trembled on his arm, and Maxwell was a little at a loss, though anxious not to seem unresponsive to Virginia's enthusiasm for spiritual vision.

"I feel that my first attention has to be given to the simpler problems, here in Durford," he replied. "But I am glad if I haven't been dull, in the process."

"Dull? No indeed—how can you say that! To my life—you will understand?" (she glanced up with tremulous flutter of eyelids) "—you have brought so much helpfulness and—and warmth." She sighed eloquently.

Maxwell was no egotist, and was always prone to see only an impersonal significance in parish compliments. A more self-conscious subject for confidences would have replied less openly.

"I am glad—very glad. But you must not think that the help has been one-sided. You have seconded my efforts so energetically—indeed I don't know what I could have accomplished without such whole-hearted help as you and Mrs. Burke and others have given."

To the optimistic Virginia the division of the loaves and fishes of his personal gratitude was scarcely heeded. She cherished her own portion, and soon magnified it to a basketful—and soon, again, to a monopoly of the entire supply. As he gave her his hand at the door of Willow Bluff, she was in fit state to invest that common act of friendliness with symbolic significance of a rosy future.

CHAPTER VII
HEPSEY GOES A-FISHING

Mrs. Burke seemed incapable of sitting still, with folded hands, for any length of time; and when the stress of her attention to household work, and her devotion to neighborly good deeds relaxed, she turned to knitting wash-rags as a sportsman turns to his gun, or a toper to his cups. She seemed to find more stimulus for thought and more helpful diversion in the production of one wash-rag than most persons find in a trip abroad.

One day, not very long after the eventful missionary tea, she was sitting in her garden, and knitting more rapidly than usual, as she said to Maxwell:

"What's been the matter with you these last few weeks? You've been lookin' altogether too sober, and you don't eat nothin' to speak of. It must be either liver, or conscience, or heart."

Secretly, she strongly suspected a cardiac affection, of the romantic variety. She intended to investigate.

Donald laughed as he replied:

"Perhaps it's all three together; but I'm all right. There's nothing the matter with me. Every man has his blue days, you know."

"Yes, but the last month you've had too many; and there must be some reason for it. There's nothin' so refreshin' as gettin' away from your best friends, once in a while. I guess you need a change—pinin' for the city, maybe. Sakes alive! I can't see how folks can live that way—all crowded up together, like a lot of prisons."

"You don't care to visit in the city, then?"

"Not on your life!"

"But a change is good for everyone. Don't you ever get away from Durford for a few weeks?"

"Not very often. What with decidin' where to go, and fussin' to get ready, and shuttin' up the house, it's more trouble than its worth. Then there's so many things to 'tend to when you get home."

"But don't you ever visit relatives?"

"Not on your life, unless I'm subpœna-ed by the coroner: though of course we do get together to celebrate a family funeral or a wedding now and then. Visitin' is no joke, I tell you. No sir, I'm old enough to know when I'm well off, and home's the best place for me. I want my own table, and my own bed when it comes night." She paused, and then remarked meditatively:

"I went down to visit in New York once."

"Didn't you enjoy your visit?" Maxwell inquired. "New York's my home-city."

"Can't say I did, awful much. You see, I was visitin' Sally Ramsdale—Sally Greenway that was. They were livin' in an apartment, ninth floor up. In the first place, I didn't like goin' up stairs in the elevator. I was so scared, I felt as if the end had come, and I was bein' jerked to my reward in an iron birdcage with a small kid dressed in brass buttons. When I got into the hall it was about two feet wide and darker than Pharaoh's conscience. It had a string of cells along the side, and one opened into a chimney, and the rest into nothin' in particular. The middle cell was a dinin' room where we ate when we could find the way to our mouths. Near as I can recollect, you got into the parlor through the pantry, back of the servant's room, by jumpin' over five trunks. You ought to have seen my room. It looked just like a parlor when you first went in. There was somethin' lookin' like a cross between an upright piano and writin' desk. Sally gave it a twist, and it tumbled out into a folding bed. The first night, I laid awake with my eyes on the foot of that bed expectin' it to rise and stand me on my head; but it didn't. You took the book of poems off the center table, gave it a flop, and it was a washstand. Everything seemed to shut up into something else it hadn't ought to. It was a 'now you see it, and now you don't see it,' kind of a room; and I seemed to be foldin' and unfoldin' most of the time. Then the ceilin' was so low that you could hardly get the cover off the soap dish. I felt all the while as if I should smother. My! but I was glad to get home and get a breath of real air."

"Yes," Maxwell replied, "people live more natural and healthful lives in the country. The advantages of the city aren't an unmixed blessing."

"That's true enough. That's no way to live. Just think of havin' no yard but a window box and a fire escape! I'd smother!

"We folks out here in the country 'aint enjoyin' a lot of the refinements of city life; anyhow we get along, and the funny part about it is,—it 'aint hard to do, either. In the first place we 'aint so particular, which helps a lot, and besides, as Jonathan Jackson used to say,—there's compensations. I had one look at Fifth Avenue and I'm not sayin' it wasn't all I had heard it was; but if I had to look at it three hundred and sixty-five days a year I wouldn't trade it for this.

"Why, some days it rains up here, but I can sit at my window and look down the valley, to where the creek runs through, and 'way up into the timber, and the sight of all those green things, livin' and noddin' in the rain is a long ways from being disheartenin',—and when the sun shines I can sit out here, in my garden, with my flowers, and watch the boys playin' down in the meadow, Bascom's Holsteins grazin' over there on the hill, and the air full of the perfume of growin' things,—they 'aint got anything like that, in New York."

For a time Mrs. Burke relapsed into silence, while Maxwell smoked his briar pipe as he lay on the grass near by. She realized that the parson had cleverly side-tracked her original subject of conversation, and as she glanced down at him she shook her head with droll deprecation of his guile.

When she first accused him of the blues, it was true that Maxwell's look had expressed glum depression. Now, he was smiling, and, balked of her prey, Mrs. Burke knitted briskly, contemplating other means drawing him from his covert. Her strategy had been too subtle: she would try a frontal attack.

"Ever think of gettin' married, Mr. Maxwell?" she inquired abruptly.

For an instant Maxwell colored; but he blew two or three rings of smoke in the air, and then replied carelessly, as he plucked at the grass by his side:

"Oh, yes: every fellow of my age has fancied himself in love some time or other, I suppose."

"Yes, it's like measles, or whoopin'-cough; every man has to have it sometime; but you haven't answered my question."

"Well, suppose I was in love; a man must be pretty conceited to imagine that he could make up to a girl for the sacrifice of bringing her to live in a place like Durford. That sounds horribly rude to Durford, but you won't misunderstand me."

"No; I know exactly how you feel; but the average girl is just dyin' to make a great sacrifice for some good-lookin' young fellow, all the same."

"Ah yes; the *average* girl; but—"

Maxwell's voice trailed off into silence, while he affected to gaze stonily into the blue deeps of the sky overhead.

Hepsey had thought herself a pretty clever fisherman, in her day; evidently, she decided, this particular fish was not going to be easy to land.

"Don't you think a clergyman is better off married?" she asked, presently.

Donald knocked the ashes out of his pipe and put it in his pocket, clasped his hands across his knees, and smiled thoughtfully for a moment. There was a light in his eyes which was good to see, and a slight trembling of his lips before he ventured to speak. Then he sighed heavily.

"Yes, I do, on many accounts. But I think that any parson in a place like this ought to know and face all the difficulties of the situation before he comes to a definite decision and marries. Isn't that your own view? You've had experience of married parsons here: what do you think?"

"Well, you see the matter is just like this: Every parish wants an unmarried parson; the vestry 'cause he's cheap, every unmarried woman 'cause he may be a possible suitor; and it's easier to run him than it is a married man. He may be decent, well-bred and educated. And he comes to a parcel of ignoramuses who think they know ten times as much as he does. If he can't earn enough to marry on, and has the good sense to keep out of matrimony, the people talk about his bein' a selfish old bachelor who neglects his duty to society. He can't afford to run a tumble-down rectory like ours. If in the face of all this he marries, he has to scrimp and stint until it is a question of buyin' one egg or two, and lettin' his wife worry and work until she's fit for a lunatic asylum. No business corporation, not even a milk-peddlin' trust, would treat its men so or expect good work from 'em. Then the average layman seldom thinks how he can help the parson. His one idea is to be a kicker as long as he can think of anything to kick about. The only man in this parish who never kicks is paralyzed in both legs. Yes sir; the parson of the country parish is the parish goat, as the sayin' is."

Mrs. Burke ceased her tirade, and after a while Maxwell remarked quietly:

"Mrs. Burke, I'm afraid you are a pessimist."

"I'm no such thing," she retorted hotly. "A pessimist's a man that sees nothin' but the bad, and says there's no help for it and won't raise a hand: he's a proper sour-belly. An optimist's a man that sees nothin' but the good, and says everything's all right; let's have a good time. Poor fool! The practical man—anyway, the practical woman—sees both the bad and the good, and says we can make things a whole lot better if we try; let's take off our coats and hustle to beat the cars, and see what happens. The real pessimists are your Bascoms, and that kind: and I guess I pity him more than blame him: he seems as lonesome as a tooth-pick in a cider-barrel."

"But I thought that Bascom was a wealthy man. He ought to be able to help out, and raise money enough so that the town could keep a parson and his wife comfortably."

"Sure thing! But the church isn't supported by tight-fisted wealthy people. It's the hard-workin' middle class who are willin' to turn in and spend their last cent for the church. And don't you get me started on Bascom as you value your life. Maybe I'll swear a blue streak before I get through: not but what I suppose that even Bascom has his good points—like a porcupine. But a little emery paper on Bascom's good points wouldn't hurt 'em very much. They're awful rusty."

"Oh well! Money isn't all there is in life," soothed Maxwell, smiling.

"No, not quite; but it's a mighty good thing to have in the house. You'd think so if you had to wear the same hat three summers. I've got to that time in my life where I can get along very well without most of the necessities; but I must have a few luxuries to keep me goin'."

"Then you think that a clergyman ought not to marry and bring his wife to a place like Durford?"

"I didn't say anything of the sort. If you was to get married I'd see you through, if it broke my neck or Bascom's."

"Do you know, you seem to me a bit illogical?" remarked Maxwell mildly.

"Don't talk to me about logic! The strongest argument is often the biggest lie. There are times in your life when you have to take your fate in both hands and shut your eyes, and jump in the dark. Maybe you'll land on your feet, and maybe you—won't. But you have got to jump just the same. That's matrimony—common sense, idiocy, or whatever you choose to call it.... I never could tell which. It's the only thing to do; and any man with a backbone and a fist won't hesitate very long. If you marry, I'll see you through; though of course you won't stay here long, anyhow."

"You're awfully kind, Mrs. Burke," Maxwell replied, "and I sha'n't forget your promise—when the time comes for me to take the momentous step. But I think it would be the wisest thing for me to keep my heart free for a while; or at any rate, not to get married."

Mrs. Burke looked down at her rector, and smiled broadly at his clever evasion of the bait she had dangled before him so persistently.

"Well, do as you like; but that reminds me that when next you go to town you'll need to get a new glass for that miniature of your sister. You must have dozed off with it in your hands last night and dropped it. I found it this morning on the floor alongside of your chair, with the glass broken."

She rose triumphantly, as she knitted the last stitch of the wash-rag. "Excuse me—I must go and peel the potatoes for dinner."

"I'd offer to contribute to the menu, by catching some fish for you; but I don't think it's a very good day for fishing, is it, Mrs. Burke?" asked Maxwell innocently.

CHAPTER VII
AN ICEBOX FOR CHERUBIM

As we have seen, when Maxwell began his work in Durford, he was full of the enthusiasm of youth and inexperience. He was, however, heartily supported and encouraged in his efforts by all but Sylvester Bascom. Without being actively and openly hostile, the Senior Warden, under the guise of superior wisdom and a judicial regard for expediency, managed to thwart many of his projects. After each interview with Bascom, Maxwell felt that every bit of life and heart had been pumped out of him, and that he was very young, and very foolish to attempt to make any change in "the good old ways" of the parish, which for so many years had stunted its growth and had acquired the immobility of the laws of the Medes and Persians.

But there was one parishioner who was ever ready to suggest new ventures to "elevate" the people, and to play the part of intimate friend and adviser to her good-looking rector, and that was Virginia Bascom. For some unknown reason "the people" did not seem to be acutely anxious thus to be elevated; and most of them seemed to regard Virginia as a harmless idiot with good intentions, but with positive genius for meddling in other people's affairs. Being the only daughter of the Senior Warden, and the leading lady from a social standpoint, she considered that she had a roving commission to set people right at a moment's notice; and there were comparatively few people in Durford on whom she had not experimented in one way or another. She organized a Browning club to keep the factory girls out of the streets evenings, a mothers' meeting, an ethical culture society, and a craftman's club, and, as she was made president of each, her time was quite well filled.

And now in her fertile brain dawned a brilliant idea, which she proceeded to propound to the rector. Maxwell was non-committal, for he felt the matter was one for feminine judgment. Then she decided to consult Mrs. Burke—because, while Hepsey was "not in society," she was recognized as the dominant personality among the women of the village, and no parish enterprise amounted to much unless she approved of it, and was gracious enough to assist. As Virginia told Maxwell, "Mrs. Burke has a talent of persuasiveness," and so was "useful in any emergency." If Mrs. Burke's sympathies could be enlisted on behalf of the new scheme it would be bound to succeed.

As a matter of fact, Mrs. Burke had heard rumors of this new project of Virginia's. It always went against the grain with Hepsey to say: "Don't do it." She was a firm believer in the teaching of experience: "Experience does it," was her translation of the classic adage.

And so one morning found Virginia sitting opposite Mrs. Burke in the kitchen at Thunder Cliff, knitting her brows and poking the toe of her boot with the end of her parasol in an absent-minded way. This was symptomatic.

"Anything on your mind, Virginia? What's up now?" Mrs. Burke began.

For a moment Virginia hesitated, and then replied:

"I am thinking of establishing a day-nursery to care for the babies of working women, Mrs. Burke."

Mrs. Burke, with hands on her hips, gazed intently at her visitor, pushed up her under lip, scowled, and then observed thoughtfully:

"I wonder some one hasn't thought of that before. Who's to take care of the babies?"

"Mary Quinn and I, with the assistance of others, of course."

"Are you sure that you know which is the business end of a nursing-bottle? Could you put a safety-pin where it would do the most good? Could you wash a baby without drownin' it?"

"Of course I have not had much experience," Virginia replied in a dignified and lofty way, "but Mary Quinn has, and she could teach me."

"You're thinkin', I suppose, that a day-nursery would fill a long-felt want, or somethin' like that. Who's goin' to pay the bills?"

"Oh, there ought to be enough progressive, philanthropic people in Durford to subscribe the necessary funds, you know. It is to be an auxiliary to the parish work."

"Hm! What does Mr. Maxwell say?"

"Well, he said that he supposed that babies were good things in their way; but he hadn't seen many in the village, and he didn't quite realize what help a day-nursery would be to the working women."

"That doesn't sound mighty enthusiastic. Maybe we might get the money; but who's to subscribe the babies?"

"Why, the working women, of course."

"They can't subscribe 'em if they haven't got 'em. There are mighty few kids in this town; and if you really want my candid opinion, I don't think Durford needs a day-nursery any more than it needs an icebox for cherubim. But then of course that doesn't matter much. When you goin' to begin?"

"Next Monday. We have rented the store where Elkin's grocery used to be, and we are going to fit it up with cribs, and all the most up-to-date conveniences for a sanitary day-nursery."

"Hm! Well, I'll do all I can to help you, of course. I suppose you'll find babies pushin' all over the sidewalk Monday mornin', comin' early to avoid the rush. Better get down as early as possible, Virginia."

Virginia departed.

After the furnishing of the incipient nursery had been completed, and each little crib had a new unbreakable doll whose cheeks were decorated with unsuckable paint, Virginia and Mary Quinn—invaluable in undertaking the spadework of all Virginia's parish exploits—gave an afternoon tea to which all the subscribers and their friends were invited. But when everything was in readiness for patronage, what few working women there were in Durford, possessed of the right kind of babies, seemed strangely reluctant to trust their youthful offspring to the tender mercies of Virginia Bascom and Mary Quinn.

Consequently, the philanthropic movement, started under such favorable patronage, soon reached a critical stage in its career, and Mrs. Burke was called in to contribute some practical suggestions. She responded to the summons with all due promptness, and when she arrived at the nursery, she smilingly remarked:

"Hm! But where are the babies? I thought they would be swarming all over the place like tadpoles in a pool."

"Well, you see," Virginia began, her voice quivering with disappointment, "Mary Quinn and I have been sitting here four mortal days, and not a single infant has appeared on the scene. I must say that the working women of Durford seem strangely unappreciative of our efforts to help them."

"Well," Mrs. Burke responded, "I suppose day-nurseries without babies are as incomplete as an incubator without eggs. But after all, it hardly seems worth while to go out and snatch nursing infants from their mother's breasts just to fill a long-felt want, does it? Besides, you might get yourself into trouble."

"I didn't ask you to come and make fun of me," Virginia replied touchily. "I wanted you to make some suggestions to help us out. If we don't get any babies, we might just as well close our doors at once. I should be awfully mortified to have the whole thing a failure, after all we have done, and all the advertising we have had."

Mrs. Burke sat down and assumed a very judicial expression.

"Well, Ginty dear, I'm awful sorry for you; I don't doubt you done the best you could. It'd be unreasonable to expect you to collect babies like mushrooms in a single night. All true reformers are bound to strike snags, and to suffer because they aint appreciated in their own day and generation. It's only after we are gone and others take our places that the things we do are appreciated. You'll have to resign yourself to fate, Virginia, and wait for what the newspapers call 'the vindicatin' verdict of prosperity.' Think of all the people that tried to do things and didn't do 'em. Now there's the Christian martyrs—"

For some reason Virginia seemed to have a vague suspicion that Hepsey was still making fun of her; and being considerably nettled, she interjected tartly:

"I'm not working for the verdict of posterity, and I don't care a flip for the Christian martyrs. I'm trying to conduct a day-nursery, here and now; we have the beds, and the equipment, and some money, and—"

"But you haven't got the babies, Virginia!"

"Precisely, Mrs. Burke. It's simply a question of babies, now or never. Babies we must have or close our doors. I must confess that I am greatly pained at the lack of interest of the community in our humble efforts to serve them."

For some time Hepsey sat in silence; then she smiled as if a bright idea occurred to her.

"Why not borrow a few babies from the mothers in town, Virginia? You see, you might offer to pay a small rental by the hour, or take out a lease which could be renewed when it expired. What is lacking is public confidence in your enterprise. If you and Miss Quinn could be seen in the nursery windows dandlin' a baby on each arm, and singin' lullabies to 'em for a few days, it'd attract attention, inspire faith in the timid, and public confidence would be restored. The tide of babies'd turn your way after a while, and the nursery would prove a howlin' success."

Virginia considered the suggestion and, after deep thought, remarked:

"What do you think we ought to pay for the loan of a baby per hour, Mrs. Burke?"

"Well, of course I haven't had much experience rentin' babies, as I have been busy payin' taxes and insurance on my own for some years; then you see rents have gone up like everything lately. But I should think that ten cents an afternoon ought to be sufficient. I think I might be able to hunt up a baby or two. Mrs. Warren might lend her baby, and perhaps Mrs. Fletcher might add her twins. I'll call on them at once, if you say so."

Virginia looked relieved, and in a voice of gratitude responded:

"You are really very, very kind."

"Well, cheer up, Virginia; cheer up. Every cloud has its silver linin'; and I guess we can find some babies somewhere even if we have to advertise in the papers. Now I must be goin', and I'll stop on the way and make a bid for the Fletcher twins. Good-by."

When Nicholas Burke learned from his mother of the quest of the necessary babies, he started out of his own motion and was the first to arrive on the scene with the spoils of victory, in the shape of the eighteen-months infant of Mrs. Thomas McCarthy, for which he had been obliged to pay twenty-five cents in advance, the infant protesting vigorously with all the power of a well developed pair of lungs. As Nickey delivered the goods, he remarked casually:

"Say, Miss Virginia, you just take the darn thing quick. He's been howlin' to beat the band."

"Why, Nickey," exclaimed Virginia, entranced, and gingerly possessing herself of James McCarthy, "however did you get him?"

"His ma wouldn't let me have him at first; and it took an awful lot of jollyin' to bring her round. Of course I didn't mean to tell no lies, but I said you was awful fond of kids. I said that if you only had Jimmy, it would give the nursery a dandy send-off, 'cause she was so well known, and Mr. McCarthy was such a prominent citizen. When she saw me cough up a quarter and play with it right under her nose, I could see she was givin' in; and she says to me, 'Nickey, you can take him just this once. I'd like to help the good cause along, and Miss Bascom, she means well.' Ma's gettin' after the Fletcher twins for you."

James McCarthy was welcomed with open arms, was washed and dressed in the most approved antiseptic manner; his gums were swabed with boracic acid, and he was fed from a sterilized bottle on Pasteurized milk, and tucked up in a crib with carbolized sheets, and placed close to the window where he could bask in actinic rays, and inhale ozone to his heart's content. Thus the passer-by could see at a glance that the good work had begun to bear fruit.

Mrs. Burke managed to get hold of the Fletcher twins, and as they both howled lustily in unison, all the time, they added much to the natural domesticity of the scene and seemed to invite further patronage, like barkers at a side-show. Mrs. Warren was also persuaded.

Although the village was thoroughly canvassed, Miss Bascom was obliged to content herself with the McCarthy baby and the Fletcher twins, and the Warren baby, until, one morning, a colored woman appeared with a bundle in her arms. As she was the first voluntary contributor of live stock, she was warmly welcomed, and a great fuss made over the tiny black infant which gradually emerged from the folds of an old shawl "like a cuckoo out of its cocoon," as Mary Quinn remarked. This, of course, was very nice and encouraging, but most unfortunately, when night came, the mother did not appear to claim her progeny, nor did she ever turn up again. Of course it was a mere oversight on her part, but Virginia was much disturbed, for, to her very great embarrassment, she found herself the undisputed possessor of a coal black baby. She was horrified beyond measure, and sent at once for Mrs. Burke.

"What shall I do, what shall I do, Mrs. Burke?" she cried. Mrs. Burke gazed musingly at the writhing black blot on the white and rose blanket, and suggested:

"Pity you couldn't adopt it, Virginia. You always loved children."

"Adopt it!" Virginia screamed hysterically. "What in the world can you be thinking of?"

"Well, I can't think of anything else, unless I can persuade Andy Johnston, the colored man on the farm, to adopt it. He wouldn't mind its complexion as much as you seem to."

Virginia brightened considerably at this suggestion, exclaiming excitedly:

"Oh Mrs. Burke, do you really think you could?"

"Well, I don't know. Perhaps so. At any rate, if we offer to help pay the extra expense, Mrs. Johnston might bring the baby up as her own. Then they can name it Virginia Bascom Johnston, you see."

Virginia bit her lip, but she managed to control her temper as she exclaimed quite cheerfully:

"Mrs. Burke, you are so very kind. You are always helping somebody out of a scrape."

"Don't overpraise me, Virginia. My head's easily turned. The teachin's of experience are hard—but I guess they're best in the end. Well, send the poor little imp of darkness round to me to-night, and I'll see that it has good care."

As a matter of fact, Hepsey had qualms of conscience as to whether she should not, at the outset, have discouraged the whole baby project; experience threatened to give its lesson by pretty hard knocks, on this occasion.

For though the immediate problem was thus easily solved, others presented themselves to vex the philanthropic Virginia.

When on the tenth day the rental for the Warren baby and the Fletcher twins fell due, and the lease of James McCarthy expired without privilege of renewal, the finances of the nursery were at a very low ebb. It certainly did not help matters much when, towards night, Mary Quinn called Virginia's attention to the fact that there were unmistakable signs of a bad rash on the faces of the twins, and very suspicious spots on the cheeks of the Warren baby. Even the antiseptic James McCarthy blushed like a boiled lobster, and went hopelessly back on his sterilized character. Of course the only thing to be done was to send at once for the doctor, and for the mothers of the respective infants. When the doctor arrived he pronounced the trouble to be measles; and when the mothers made their appearance, Virginia learned something of the unsuspected resources of the English language served hot from the tongues of three frightened and irate women. Finally the floor was cleared, and the place closed up for disinfection.

Just before she left, Virginia dropped into a chair and wept, quite oblivious of the well-meant consolations of Mary Quinn, sometime co-partner in "The Durford Day-Nursery for the Children of Working Women."

"We've done the very best we could, Miss Bascom; and it certainly isn't our fault that the venture turned out badly. Poor babies!"

At this the sobbing Virginia was roused to one last protest:

"Mary Quinn, if ever you say another word to me about babies, I'll have you arrested. I just hate babies, and—and everything! Why, there comes Mr. Maxwell! Say, Mary, you just run and get me a wet towel to wipe my face with, while I hunt for my combs and do up my back hair. And then if you wouldn't mind vanishing for a while—I'm sure you understand—for if ever I needed spiritual consolation and the help of the church, it is now, this minute."

CHAPTER IX

THE RECTORY

A few weeks after Donald's conversational duel with Mrs. Burke he started on a six-weeks' vacation, which he had certainly earned; and as he busied himself with his packing,—Hepsey assisting,—he announced:

"When I come back, Mrs. Burke, I probably shall not come alone."

He was strapping up his suit-case when he made this rather startling announcement, and the effect seemed to send the blood to his head. Mrs. Burke did not seem to notice his confusion as she remarked calmly:

"Hm! That's a good thing. Your grandmother can have the room next to yours, and we'll do all we can to make the old lady comfortable. I'm sure she'll be a great comfort to you, though she'll get a bit lonesome at times, unless she's active on her feet."

Donald laughed, as he blushed more furiously and stuttered:

"No, I am not going to bring my grandmother here, and I strongly suspect that you know what I mean. I'm going to be married."

"So you are going to get married, are you?" Hepsey remarked with due amazement, as if the suspicion of the fact had never entered her head before. "Well, I am mighty glad of it. I only wish that I was goin' to be present to give you away. Yes, I'm mighty glad. She'll make a new man of you up here, so long as she isn't a new woman."

"No, not in the slang sense of the word; although I think you will find her very capable, and I hope with all my heart that you'll like her."

"I'm sure I shall. The question is whether she'll like me."

Hepsey Burke looked rather sober for a moment, and Donald instantly asserted:

"She can't help liking you."

"We-ell now, I could mention quite a number of people who find it as easy as rolling off a log to *dis*like, me. But that doesn't matter much. I have found it a pretty good plan not to expect a great deal of adoration, and to be mighty grateful for the little you get. Be sure you let me know when to expect you and your grandmother back."

"Most certainly I shall," he laughed. "It will be in about six weeks, you know. Good-by, and thank you a thousand times for all your kindness to me."

There was considerable moisture in Hepsey's eyes as she stood and watched Maxwell drive down the road. Then wiping her eyes furtively with one corner of her apron she remarked to herself:

"Well, I suppose I am glad, mighty glad; but somehow it isn't the jolliest thing in the world to have one's friends get married. They are never the same again; and in ten times out of six the lady in the case is jealous of her husband's friends, and tries to make trouble. It takes a lady saint to share her husband's interests with anybody, and maybe she 'aint to blame. Well, the next thing in order is to fix up the rectory in six weeks. The best way to repair that thing is with a match and some real good kerosene and a few shavings; however, we'll have to do the best we can. I think I'll set Jonathan Jackson to work this afternoon, and go around and interview the vestry myself."

Jonathan proved resignedly obedient to Hepsey's demands, but the vestry blustered and scolded, because they had not been consulted in the matter, until Hepsey said she would be glad to receive any contribution they might choose to offer; then they relapsed into innocuous desuetude and talked crops.

As soon as the repairs were well under way, the whole town was wild with gossip about Maxwell and Miss Bascom. If he were going to occupy the rectory, the necessary inference was that he was going to be married, as he surely would not contemplate keeping bachelor's hall by himself. At last Virginia had attained the height of her ambition and captured the rector! Consequently she was the center of interest in every social gathering, although, as the engagement had not been formally announced, no one felt at liberty to congratulate her. To any tentative and insinuating advances in this direction Virginia replied by non-committal smiles, capable of almost any interpretation; and the seeker after information was none the wiser.

Mrs. Roscoe-Jones, by virtue of her long intimacy with Hepsey and her assured social position in Durford's thirty gentry, felt that she was entitled to some definite information; and so, as they walked back from church one Wednesday afternoon, she remarked:

"I hear that the parish is going to repair the rectory, and that you are taking a great interest in it. You must be on very intimate terms with Mr. Bascom and the vestry!"

"Well, not exactly. Bascom and I haven't held hands in the dark for some time; but I am going to do what I can to get the house in order for Mr. Maxwell."

"I wonder where the money is coming from to complete the work? It seems to me that the whole parish ought to be informed about the matter, and share in the work; but I suppose Mr. Bascom's shouldering it all, since there's been no effort to raise money by having a fair."

"I really don't know much about it as yet, Sarah. Of course Bascom's charitable work is mostly done in secret, so that nobody ever finds it out. He is a modest man and wouldn't like to be caught in the act of signing a check for anybody else. It might seem showy."

"Yes, I understand," Mrs. Roscoe-Jones retorted dryly; "but under the circumstances, that is—"

"Under what circumstances?" Mrs. Burke inquired quickly.

"Oh, considering that Mr. Bascom is Virginia's father and would want to make her comfortable, you know—"

"No, I don't know. I'm awful stupid about some things. You must have discovered that before."

"Now Hepsey, what is the use of beating around the bush like this? You must know the common gossip of the town, and you must be in Mr. Maxwell's confidence. What shall I say when people ask me if he is engaged to Virginia Bascom?"

"Tell 'em you don't know a blessed thing about it. What else can you tell 'em? You might tell 'em that you tried to pump me and the pump wouldn't work 'cause it needed packin'."

After this, Mrs. Roscoe-Jones felt that there was nothing left for her to do but retire from the scene; so she crossed the road.

When Mrs. Burke began the actual work on the rectory she quickly realized what she had to cope with. The workmen of Durford had a pleasing habit of accepting all offers of work, and promising anything, and making a start so as to get the job; and then, having upset the whole premises, they promptly "lit out" for parts unknown in order to get another job, and no mortal knew when they would return. It always seemed promising and hopeful to see a laboring man arrive in his overalls with his dinner-pail and tools at seven; but when two hours later he had vanished, not to return, it was a bit discouraging. Mrs. Burke was not in a very good humor when, arriving at the rectory, she met Tom Snyder the plumber, at ten-thirty, walking briskly away from his job. She planted herself squarely across the walk and began:

"Good morning, Thomas; where are you going, if I may ask?"

"I am going back for my tools, Mrs. Burke."

"Excuse me, Thomas, but you were never more mistaken in your life. You put the kitchen pipes out of business two weeks ago, and you must have been goin' back for your tools ever since. I suppose you're chargin' me by the hour for goin' backwards."

Thomas looked sheepish and scratched his head with his dirty fingers.

"No, but I have to finish a little job I begun for Elias Warden on the hill. I'll be back again right away."

"None of that, Thomas. You're goin' back to the rectory with me now, and if the job isn't finished by six o'clock, you'll never get your hands on it again."

The crestfallen Thomas reluctantly turned around and accompanied Hepsey back to the rectory and finished his work in half an hour.

After much trial and tribulation the rectory was duly repaired, replastered, and papered. The grass had been cut; the bushes were trimmed; and the house had been painted. Then Mrs. Burke obtained a hayrack with a team, and taking Nickey and Jonathan Jackson with her, made a tour of the parish asking for such furniture as individual parishioners were willing to give. Late in the afternoon she arrived at the rectory with a very large load, and the next day Jonathan was made to set to work with his tools, and she started in with some paint and varnish, and the result seemed eminently satisfactory to her, even though her hands were stained, she had had no dinner, and her hair was stuck to her head here and there in shiny spots. As they were leaving the house to return home for supper, she scowled severely at Jonathan as she remarked:

"Jonathan, I do believe you've got more red paint on the top of your head than you left on the kitchen chairs. Do for mercy sake wash the end of your nose. I don't care to be seen comin' out of here with you lookin' like that," she added scathingly.

After that, it was, as Mrs. Burke remarked, just fun to finish the rectory; and though so much had been given by the people of the parish, there were many new pieces of furniture delivered, for which no one could account. As neither Mr. Bascom nor Miss Bascom had sent anything, and as neither had appeared on the scene, excitement was at fever heat. Rumor had it that Virginia had gone to the city for a week or so, to buy her trousseau. Presently the report circulated that Maxwell was going to bring his bride back with him when he returned from his vacation.

The day before the one set for Maxwell's arrival Mrs. Burke confessed the truth, and suggested that the rectory be stocked with provisions, so that the bride and groom should have something to eat when they first got home. The idea seemed to please the parish, and provisions began to arrive and were placed in the cellar, or on the newly painted pantry shelves, or in the neat cupboards. Mrs. Talbot sent a bushel of potatoes, Mrs. Peterson a pan of soda biscuit, Mrs. Andrews two loaves of bread; Mrs. Squires donated a pan of soda biscuit, Mrs. Johnson some frosted cake, and Mrs. Marlow two bushels of apples. Mrs. Hurd sent a pan of soda biscuit, Mrs. Waldorf three dozen eggs, and a sack of flour; Mrs. Freyburg sent a pan of soda biscuit, Mrs. Jones a boiled ham, Mrs. Orchardson two bushels of turnips and half a pan of soda biscuit.

Mrs. Burke received the provisions as they arrived, and put them where they belonged. Just about supper time Mrs. Loomis came with a large bundle under her arm and remarked to Hepsey:

"I thought I'd bring something nobody else would think of — something out of the ordinary that perhaps Mr. and Mrs. Maxwell would relish."

"I'm sure that was real thoughtful of you, Mrs. Loomis," Hepsey replied. "What have you got?"

"Well," Mrs. Loomis responded, "I thought I'd bring 'em two pans of my nice fresh soda biscuit."

Mrs. Burke kept her face straight, and responded cheerfully:

"That was awful nice of you, Mrs. Loomis."

"Oh, that's all right. And if you want any more, just let me know."

Finally, when the door was closed on the last contributor, Mrs. Burke dropped into a chair and called:

"Jonathan Jackson, come here quick."

Jonathan responded promptly, and anxiously inquired:

"Hepsey, be you ill?"

"No, I'm not sick; but we have ten pans of soda biscuit. They are in the pantry, down cellar, in the woodshed, on the parlor table. For mercy's sake take eight pans out to the chickens or stick 'em on the picket fence. I just loathe soda biscuit; and if any more come I shall throw 'em at the head of the woman that brings 'em."

CHAPTER X
THE BRIDE'S ARRIVAL

Next morning, when Nickey brought up the mail, Mrs. Burke looked anxiously over her letters until she came to the one she was expecting. She read it in silence.

The gist of the matter was that Maxwell had been married to the nicest girl in the world, and was looking forward to having Mrs. Burke meet her, and to have his wife know the woman who had been so supremely good to him in the parish. He closed by informing her that they were to return the next day at five P. M., and if it were not asking too much, he hoped that she would take them in for a few days until they could find quarters elsewhere. The letter was countersigned by a pretty little plea for friendship from "Mrs. Betty."

Mrs. Burke replaced the letter and murmured to herself, smiling:

"Poor little dear! Of course they could come and stay as long as they pleased; but as the rectory is in order, I think that I'll meet them at the depot, and take them there direct. They'll be much happier alone by themselves from the start. I'll have supper ready for 'em, and cook the chickens while they're unpackin' their trunks."

As Mrs. Burke thought it best to maintain a discreet silence as to the time of their arrival, there was no one but herself to meet them at the station when the train pulled in. As Maxwell presented his wife to Mrs. Burke, Hepsey took the girl's two hands in hers and kissed her heartily, and then, looking at her keenly as the bride blushed under her searching gaze, she remarked:

"You're a dreadful disappointment, Mrs. Maxwell. I'm afraid it'll take me a long time to get over it."

"I am horribly sorry to disappoint you so, Mrs. Burke."

Maxwell laughed, while Mrs. Betty looked puzzled.

"Yes," Mrs. Burke continued, "you're a dreadful disappointment. Your picture isn't half as sweet as you are." Then turning to Maxwell, she said:

"Why didn't you tell me? Who taught you to pick out just the right sort of wife, I'd like to know?"

"*She* did!" Maxwell replied, pointing delightedly to the young woman, who was still smiling and blushing under Hepsey's inspection.

"But Mrs. Burke," Mrs. Betty interposed, "can't you give me a little credit for 'picking out' Donald, as you say?"

"Yes; Mr. Maxwell's pretty fine, though I wouldn't want to have you tell him so, for anything. But I know, because Durford is calculated to test a man's mettle, if any place ever was. Now Mrs. Betty, if that's what I'm to call you, if you'll get into the wagon we'll drive home and have some supper. You must be 'most famished by this time, if you stop thinkin' about Mr. Maxwell long enough to have an appetite. I suppose that we might have had a committee of the vestry down here to bid you welcome to Durford; and Nickey suggested the village band and some hot air balloons, and that the boys of the parish should pull the carriage up to the house after they'd presented you with a magnificent bouquet; but I thought you'd just like to slip in unnoticed and get acquainted with your parishioners one at a time. It'd be simply awful to have a whole bunch of 'em thrown at your head at once; and as for the whole vestry—well, never mind."

They got into the "democrat" and started out at a smart trot, but when they came to the road which turned toward Thunder Cliff, Mrs. Burke drove straight across the green.

"Why, where are you going, Mrs. Burke?" Maxwell exclaimed.

"Well, I thought that maybe Mrs. Betty would like to get a sight of the town before we went home."

When they came to the rectory and turned into the yard, the wonderful transformation dawned on Maxwell.

"My gracious, what a change! It's perfectly marvelous," he exclaimed. "Why Mrs. Burke, I believe you've brought us here to live!"

"Right you are, my friend. This is where you belong."

"Well, you certainly do beat the Dutch. Who is responsible for all this, I'd like to know? But of course it's you."

"Well, I had a hand in it, but so did the whole parish. Now walk right in and make yourselves at home."

Mrs. Burke enjoyed to the full Maxwell's surprise and delight, as he and Mrs. Betty explored the house like a couple of very enthusiastic children. When they got into the china closet and Mrs. Betty found a silver tea-ball she exclaimed rapturously:

"Look here, Donald! Did you ever see the like of this? Here is a regular tea-ball. We will have tea every afternoon at four, and Mrs. Burke will be our guest. How perfectly delightful."

This remark seemed to please Hepsey mightily, as she exclaimed:

"Oh, my, no! Do you want to spoil my nervous system? We are not given much to tea-balls in Durford. We consider ourselves lucky if we get a plain old-fashioned pot. Now you get fixed up," she directed, "while I get supper ready, and I'll stay just this time, if you'll let me, and then if you can stand it, perhaps you'll ask me again."

Soon they sat down to a little table covered with spotless linen and a pretty set of white china with gold bands. Maxwell did not say much; he was still too surprised and delighted.

"OH WELL, I ALWAYS BELIEVE THAT TWO YOUNG MARRIED PEOPLE SHOULD START OUT BY THEMSELVES, AND THEN IF THEY GET INTO A FAMILY ROW IT WON'T SCANDALIZE THE PARISH"

The broiled chickens and the browned potato balls were placed before Maxwell, who faced Mrs. Betty—Hepsey sitting between them.

"Now this is what I call rich," Maxwell exclaimed as he carved. "I hadn't the slightest suspicion that we were to come here and find all these luxuries."

"However did the house get furnished?" chimed in Mrs. Betty.

"Oh well," Mrs. Burke replied, "I always believe that two young married people should start out by themselves, you know; and then if they get into a family row it won't scandalize the parish. The only new thing about the furnishings is paint and varnish. I drove around and held up the parish, and made them stand and deliver the goods, and Jonathan Jackson and I touched it up a little; that's all."

"We ought to acknowledge each gift personally," Maxwell said. "You must tell us who's given what."

"Oh, no you won't. When I took these things away from their owners by force, I acknowledged them in the politest way possible, so as to save you the trouble. You're not supposed to know where a thing came from."

"But there must have been a lot of money spent on the rectory to get it into shape," Maxwell asserted. "Where did it all come from?"

Mrs. Burke grinned with amusement.

"Why, can't you guess? Of course it was that merry-hearted, generous old Senior Warden of yours. Who else could it be? If there is anything you need, just let us know."

"But the house seems to be very completely furnished as it is."

"No, not yet. If you look around you'll see lots of things that aren't here."

Mrs. Betty quite raved over the salad, made of lettuce, oranges, walnuts and a mayonnaise dressing. Then there came ice cream and chocolate sauce, followed by black coffee.

"This is quite too much, Mrs. Burke. You must be a superb cook. I am horribly afraid you'll have spoiled Donald, so that my cooking will seem very tame to him," Mrs. Betty remarked.

"Well, never mind, Mrs. Betty. If worst comes to worst there are seven pans of soda biscuit secreted around the premises somewhere; so don't be discouraged. There are lots of things you can do with a soda biscuit, if you know how. Now we'll just clear the table, and wash the dishes, and put things away."

When about nine o'clock she arose to go, Maxwell took both Hepsey's hands in his and said quietly:

"Mrs. Burke, I'm more indebted to you than I can possibly say, for all you have done for us. I wish I knew how to thank you properly, but I don't."

"Oh, never mind that," Mrs. Burke replied, a mist gathering in her eyes, "it's been lots of fun, and if you're satisfied I'm more than pleased." Then, putting her arm around Mrs. Betty's waist, she continued:

"Remember that we're not payin' this nice little wife of yours to do parish work, and if people interfere with her you just tell em to go to Thunder Cliff. Good-by."

She was turning away when suddenly she stopped, an expression of horror on her face:

"My! think of that now! This was a bride's dinner-party, and I put yellow flowers on the table, instead of white! What'd city folks say to that!"

CHAPTER XI
VIRGINIA'S HIGH HORSE

Mrs. Betty soon succeeded in winning a place for herself in the hearts of her parishioners, and those who called to look over her "clothes," and see if she was going to "put on airs" as a city woman, called again because they really liked her. She returned the calls with equal interest, and soon had her part of the parish organization well in hand.

Maxwell's choice was, in fact, heartily approved—except by Virginia Bascom and the Senior Warden. The former took the opportunity to leave cards on an afternoon when all Durford was busily welcoming Betty at a tea; and was "not at home" when Betty duly returned the call. Virginia was also careful not to "see" either Betty or her husband if, by any chance, they passed her when in town.

Of all of which manœuvres Betty and Donald remained apparently sublimely unconscious.

As a means of making some return for the good-hearted generosity and hospitality of the inhabitants, represented by the furniture at the rectory and many tea-parties under various roof-trees, Mrs. Maxwell persuaded her husband that they should give a parish party.

So invitations were issued broadcast, and Mrs. Burke was asked to scan the lists, lest anyone be omitted. China sufficient for the occasion was supplemented by Hepsey Burke and Jonathan Jackson, and Nickey laid his invaluable services under contribution to fetch and carry—organizing a corps of helpers.

The whole adult village,—at least the feminine portion of it,—young and old, presented themselves at the party, dressed in their best bibs and tuckers, amusing themselves outdoors at various improvised games, under the genial generalship of their host; and regaling themselves within at the tea-tables presided over by Mrs. Betty, whose pride it was to have prepared with her own hands,—assisted by the indefatigable Hepsey,—all the cakes and preserves and other confections provided for the occasion. The whole party was one whole-hearted, simply convivial gathering—with but a single note to mar it; and who knows whether the rector, and still less the rector's wife, would have noticed it, but for Hepsey Burke's subsequent "boiling over?"

When the games and feast were at full swing, Virginia Bascom's loud-voiced automobile drove up, and the door-bell pealed. The guests ceased chattering and the little maid, hired for the occasion, hurried from the tea-cups to answer the haughty summons. Through the silence in the tea-room, produced by the overpowering clatter of the bell, the voice of the little maid,—quite too familiar for the proper formality of the occasion, in Virginia's opinion,—was heard to pipe out cheerily:

"Come right in, Miss Virginia; the folks has eat most all the victuals—but I guess Mrs. Maxwell'll find ye some."

"Please announce 'Miss Virginia Bascom'," droned the lady, ignoring the untoward levity of the now cowering maid, and followed her to the door of the room full of guests, where she paused impressively.

"Mrs. Bascom," called the confused maid, through the solemn silence, as all eyes turned towards the door, "here's,—this is,—I mean Miss Virginia says Miss Virginia Maxwell—" After which confusing and somewhat embarrassing announcement the maid summarily fled to the kitchen, and left Virginia to her own devices.

Betty at once came forward, and quite ignoring the error, smiled a pleasant welcome.

"Miss Bascom, it is very nice to know you at last. We have been so unlucky, have we not?"

Virginia advanced rustling, and gave Betty a frigid finger-tip, held shoulder-high, and cast a collective stare at hostess and guests through her lorgnette, bowing to Maxwell and ignoring his proffered handshake.

There was an awkward pause. For once even Betty-the-self-possessed was at a loss for the necessary tactics.

A hearty voice soon filled the empty spaces: "Hello there, Ginty; I always did say those auto's was a poor imitation of a street-car; when they get balky and leave you sticking in the road-side and make you behind-time, you can't so much as get your fare back and walk. None but royalty, duchesses, and the four-hundred can afford to risk losing their cup o' tea in them things."

There was a general laugh at Hepsey's sally, and conversation again resumed its busy buzzing, and Virginia was obliged to realize that her entry had been something of a frost.

She spent some minutes drawing off her gloves, sipped twice at a cup of tea, and nibbled once at a cake; spent several more minutes getting her hands back into her gloves, fixed a good-by smile on her face, murmured some unintelligible words to her hostess, and departed, annoyed to realize that the engine of the awaiting car—kept running to emphasize her comet-like passage through so mixed an assembly—had become quite inaudible to the company.

"Such an insult!" stormed the lady, as she returned home in high dudgeon. "I might have been a nobody, the way they treated me. Dad shall hear of this; and I'll see that he puts them where they belong. The impudence! And after his t-treating me s-s-so!" she wept with chagrin, and malice that betokened no good to the rector and his little wife.

Even so, it is doubtful if the host and hostess would have permitted themselves to notice the supercilious rudeness of the leader of Durford "Society," had Hepsey been able to curb her indignation.

As she and Betty and the little maid, assisted by Donald and Nickey and his helpers, were clearing up the fragments that remained of the entertainment, Hepsey broke forth:

"If I don't set that young woman down in her place where she belongs before I've done, I've missed my guess: 'Please announce Miss Virginia Bascom,' indeed! If that isn't sauce, I'm the goose."

"Oh never mind, Mrs. Burke," soothed Betty in a low voice; "she'll soon realize that we're doing things in good old country style, and haven't brought any city ways with us to Durford. I dare say she thought—"

"Thought nothin'!" replied the exasperated Hepsey. "I'll thought her, with her high looks and her proud stomach, as the psalmist says. I'd like—oh, wouldn't I just like to send up a nice little basket of these left-over victuals to Ginty, 'with Mrs. Maxwell's regards.'"

She laughed heartily, but Betty was determined not to let herself dwell on anything so trivial, and soon, by way of changing the subject, she was putting Nickey up to the idea of forming a boy-scout corps, which, as she added, could present the village with a thoroughly versatile organization, both useful and ornamental.

"Gee," remarked Nickey, who quickly saw himself captaining a body of likely young blades, "that'd be some lively corpse, believe me. When can we start in, Mrs. Maxwell?"

"You must ask Mr. Maxwell all about that, Nickey," she laughed.

"But not now," interposed his mother. "You come along with me this minute, and let Mr. Maxwell have a bit of peace; I know how he just loves these teas. Good night, all!" she called as she departed with her son under her wing.

"Donald! Wasn't it all fun—and weren't they all splendid?" Betty glowed.

"More fun than a barrel of Bascoms—monkeys, I mean," he corrected himself, laughing at Betty's shocked expression.

CHAPTER XII
HOUSE CLEANING AND BACHELORHOOD

Apart from Mrs. Burke, there was no one in the town who so completely surrendered to Mrs. Maxwell's charms as Jonathan Jackson, the Junior Warden. Betty had penetration enough to see, beneath the man's rough exterior, all that was fine and lovable, and she treated him with a jolly, friendly manner that warmed his heart.

One day she and Mrs. Burke went over to call on Jonathan, and found him sitting in the woodshed on a tub turned bottom upwards, looking very forlorn and disconsolate.

"What's the matter, Jonathan? You look as if you had committed the unpardonable sin," Hepsey greeted him.

"No, it 'aint me," Jonathan replied; "it's Mary McGuire that's the confounded sinner this time."

"Well, what's Mary been up to now?"

"Mary McGuire's got one of her attacks of house-cleanin' on, and I tell you it's a bad one. Drat the nuisance."

"Why Jonathan! Don't swear like that."

"Well, I be hanged if I can stand this sort of thing much longer. Mary, she's the deuce and all, when she once gets started house-cleanin'."

"Oh dear," Mrs. Betty sympathized. "It's a bother, isnt it? But it doesn't take so long, and it will soon be over, won't it?"

"Well, I don't know as to that," replied Jonathan disconsolately. "Mary McGuire seems to think that the whole house must be turned wrong side out, and every bit of furniture I've got deposited in the front yard. Now, Mrs. Betty, you just look over there once. There's yards and yards of clothes-line covered with carpets and rugs and curtains I've been ordered to clean. It's somethin' beyond words. The whole place looks as if there was goin' to be an auction, or a rummage sale, or as if we had moved out 'cause the house was afire. Then she falls to with tubs of boilin' hot soap-suds, until it fills your lungs, and drips off the ends of your nose and your fingers, and smells like goodness knows what."

"Jonathan!" Hepsey reproved.

"Are you exaggerating just the least bit?" echoed Betty.

"No ma'am, I'm not. Words can't begin to tell the tale when Mary gets the fever on. I thought I noticed symptoms of house-cleanin' last week. Mary was eyein' things round the house, and givin' me less and less to eat, and lookin' at me with that cold-storage stare of hers that means death or house-cleanin'."

"But, Mr. Jackson," Betty pleaded, "your house has to be cleaned sometimes, you know."

"Sure thing," Jonathan replied. "But there's altogether too much of this house-cleanin' business goin' on to suit me. I don't see any dirt anywheres."

"That's because you are a man," Hepsey retorted. "Men never see dirt until they have to take a shovel to it."

Jonathan sighed hopelessly. "What's the use of bein' a widower," he continued, "if you can't even have your own way in your own house, I'd just like to know? I have to eat odds and ends of cold victuals out here in the woodshed, or anywhere Mary McGuire happens to drop 'em."

"That's tough luck, Mr. Jackson. You just come over to dinner with Donald and me and have a square meal."

"I'd like to awful well, Mrs. Maxwell, but I dasn't: if I didn't camp out and eat her cold victuals she'd laid out for me, it'd spoil the pleasure of house-cleanin' for her. 'Taint as though it was done with when she's finished, neither. After it's all over, and things are set to rights, they're all wrong. Some shades won't roll up. Some won't roll down; why, I've undressed in the dark before now, since one of 'em suddenly started rollin' up on me before I'd got into bed, and scared the wits out of me. She'll be askin' me to let her give the furnace a sponge bath next. I believe she'd use tooth-powder on the inside of a boiled egg, if she only knew how. This house-cleanin' racket is all dum nonsense, anyhow."

"Why Jonathan! Don't swear like that," Betty exclaimed laughing; "Mr. Maxwell's coming."

"I said *d-u-m*, Mrs. Betty; I never say nothin' worse than that—'cept when I lose my temper," he added, safely, examining first the hone and then the edge of the scythe, as if intending to sharpen it.

Hepsey had gone into the house to inspect for herself the thoroughness of Mary McGuire's operations; Betty thought the opportunity favorable for certain counsels.

"The trouble with you is you shouldn't be living alone, like this, Jonathan. You have all the disadvantages of a house, and none of the pleasures of a home."

"Yes," he responded, yawning, "it's true enough; but I 'aint a chicken no more, Mrs. Betty, and I've 'most forgot how to do a bit of courtin'. What with cleanin' up, and puttin' on your Sunday clothes, and goin' to the barber's, and gettin' a good ready, it's a considerable effort for an old man like me."

"I AIN'T A CHICKEN NO MORE, MRS. BETTY, AND I'VE 'MOST FORGOT HOW TO DO A BIT OF COURTIN'"

"People don't want to see your clothes; they want to see you. If you feel obliged to, you can send your Sunday clothes around some day and let her look at them once for all. Keeping young is largely a matter of looking after your digestion and getting plenty of sleep. Its all foolishness for you to talk about growing old. Why, you are in the prime of life."

"Hm! Yes. And why don't you tell me that I look real handsome, and that the girls are all crazy for me. You're an awful jollier, Mrs. Betty, though I'll admit that a little jollyin' does me a powerful lot of good now and then. I sometimes like to believe things I know to a certainty 'aint true, if they make me feel good."

For a moment Betty kept silent, gazing into the kindly face, and then the instinct of match-making asserted itself too strongly to be resisted.

"There's no sense in your being a lonesome widower. Why don't you get married? I mean it."

For a moment Jonathan was too astounded at the audacity of the serious suggestion to reply; but when he recovered his breath he exclaimed:

"Well, I swan to man! What will you ask me to be doin' next?"

"Oh, I mean it, all right," persisted Mrs. Betty. "Here you've got a nice home for a wife, and I tell you you need the happiness of a real home. You will live a whole lot longer if you have somebody to love and look after; and if you want to know what you will be asking me to do next, I will wager a box of candy it will be to come to your wedding."

"Make it cigars, Mrs. Betty; I'm not much on candy. Maybe you're up to tellin' me who'll have me. I haven't noticed any females makin' advances towards me in some time now. The only woman I see every day is Mary McGuire, and she'd make a pan-cake griddle have the blues if she looked at it."

Mrs. Betty grasped her elbow with one hand, and putting the first finger of the other hand along the side of her little nose, whispered:

"What's the matter with Mrs. Burke?"

Jonathan deliberately pulled a hair from his small remaining crop and cut it with the scythe, as if he had not heard Betty's impertinent suggestion. But finally he replied:

"There's nothin' the matter with Mrs. Burke that I know of; but that's no reason why she should be wantin' to marry me."

"She thinks a great deal of you; I know she does."

"How do you know she does?"

"Well, I heard her say something very nice about you yesterday."

"Hm! Did you? What was it?"

"She said that you were the most—the most economical man she ever met."

"Sure she didn't say I was tighter than the bark on a tree? I guess I 'aint buyin' no weddin' ring on the strength of that. Now, Mrs. Betty, you just try again. I guess you're fooling me!"

"Oh no, really I'm not. I never was more serious in my life. I mean just what I say. I know Mrs. Burke really thinks a very great deal of you, and if you like her, you ought to propose to her. Every moment a man remains single is an outrageous waste of time."

Jonathan grinned as he retorted:

"Well, no man would waste any time if all the girls were like you. They'd all be comin' early to avoid the rush. Is Mrs. Burke employin' your services as a matrimonial agent? Maybe you won't mind tellin' me what you're to get if the deal pulls off. Is there a rake-off anywheres?"

Betty laughed, and Jonathan was silent for a while, squinting at the scythe-edge, first from one angle, then from another, and tentatively raising the hone as if to start sharpening.

"Well, Mrs. Betty," he said presently, "seein' I can't possibly marry you, I don't mind tellin' you that I think the next best thing would be to marry Hepsey Burke. She's been a mighty good friend and neighbor ever since my wife died; but she wouldn't look at the likes of me. 'Twouldn't be the least use of proposin' to her."

"How do you know it wouldn't? You are not afraid of proposing, are you?"

"No, of course not; but I can't run over and propose, as I would ask her to lend me some clothes-line. That'd be too sudden; and courtin' takes a lot of time and trouble. I guess I 'most forgot how by this time; and then, to tell you the truth, I always was a bit shy. It took me near onto five years to work myself up to the sticking point when I proposed to my first wife."

"Well, now that's easy enough; Mrs. Burke usually sits on the side porch after supper with her knitting. Why don't you drop over occasionally, and approach the matter gradually? It wouldn't take long to work up to the point."

"But how shall I begin? I guess you'll have to give me lessons."

"Oh, make her think you are very lonely. Pity is akin to love, you know."

"But she knows well enough I'm mighty lonely at times. That won't do."

"Then make her think that you are a regular daredevil, and are going to the bad. Maybe she'll marry you to save you."

"Me, goin' to the bad at my age, and the Junior Warden of the church, too. What are you thinkin' of?"

"It is never too late to mend, you know. You might try being a little frisky, and see what happens."

"Oh, I know what would happen all right. She'd be over here in two jerks of a lamb's tail, and read the riot act, and scare me out of a year's growth. Hepsey's not a little thing to be playin' with."

"Well, you just make a start. Anything to make a start, and the rest will come easy."

"My, how the neighbors'd talk!"

"Talk is cheap; and besides, in a quiet place like this it's a positive duty to afford your neighbors some diversion; you ought to be thankful. You'll become a public benefactor. Now will you go ahead?"

"Mrs. Betty, worry's bad for the nerves, and's apt to produce insomny and neurastheny. But I'll think it over—yes, I will—I'll think it over."

Whereupon he suddenly began to whet his scythe with such vim as positively startled Betty.

CHAPTER XIII
THE CIRCUS

The Maxwells were, in fact, effectively stirring up the ambitions of their flock, routing the older members out of a too easy-going acceptance of things-as-they-are, and giving to the younger ones vistas of a life imbued with more color and variety than had hitherto entered their consciousness. And yet it happened at Durford, on occasion, that this awakening of new talents and individuality produced unlocked for complications.

"Oh yes," Hepsey remarked one day to Mrs. Betty, when the subject of conversation had turned to Mrs. Burke's son and heir, "Nickey means to be a good boy, but he's as restless as a kitten on a hot Johnny-cake. He isn't a bit vicious, but he do run his heels down at the corners, and he's awful wearin' on his pants-bottoms and keeps me patchin' and mendin' most of the time—'contributing to the end in view,' as Abraham Lincoln said. But, woman-like, I guess he finds the warmest spot in my heart when I'm doin' some sort of repairin' on him or his clothes. It would be easier if his intentions wasn't so good, 'cause I could spank him with a clear conscience if he was vicious. But after all, Nickey seems to have a winnin' way about him. He knows every farmer within three miles; he'll stop any team he meets, climb into the wagon seat, take the reins, and enjoy himself to his heart's content. All the men seem to like him and give in to him;

more's the pity! And he seems to just naturally lead the other kids in their games and mischief."

"Oh well, I wouldn't give a cent for a boy who didn't get into mischief sometimes," consoled Mrs. Betty.

At which valuation Nickey was then in process of putting himself and his young friends at a premium. For, about this time, in their efforts to amuse themselves, Nickey and some of his friends constructed a circus ring back of the barn: After organizing a stock company and conducting several rehearsals, the rest of the boys in the neighborhood were invited to form an audience, and take seats which had been reserved for them without extra charge on an adjoining lumber pile. Besides the regular artists there were a number of specialists or "freaks," who added much to the interest and excitement of the show.

For example, Sam Cooley, attired in one of Mrs. Burke's discarded underskirts, filched from the ragbag, with some dried cornstalk gummed on his face, impersonated the famous Bearded Lady from Hoboken.

Billy Burns, wearing a very hot and stuffy pillow buttoned under his coat and thrust down into his trousers, represented the world-renowned Fat Man from Spoonville. His was rather a difficult role to fill gracefully, because the squashy pillow would persist in bulging out between his trousers and his coat in a most indecent manner; and it kept him busy most of the time tucking it in.

Dimple Perkins took the part of the Snake Charmer from Brooklyn, and at intervals wrestled fearlessly with a short piece of garden hose which was labeled on the bills as an "Anna Condy." This he wound around his neck in the most reckless manner possible; it was quite enough to make one's blood run cold to watch him.

The King of the Cannibal Islands was draped in a buffalo robe, with a gilt paper crown adorning his head, and a very suggestive mutton-bone in his hand.

Poor little Herman Amdursky was selected for the Living Skeleton, because of the spindle-like character of his nethermost limbs. He had to remove his trousers and his coat, and submit to having his ribs wound with yards of torn sheeting, in order that what little flesh he had might be compressed to the smallest possible compass. The result was astonishingly satisfactory.

The Wild Man from Borneo wore his clothes wrong side out, as it is well known wild men from Borneo always do; and he ate grass with avidity. Wry-mouthed and squint-eyed, he was the incarnation of the cubist ideal.

When all this splendid array of talent issued from the dressing-room and marched triumphantly around the ring, it was indeed a proud moment in the annals of Durford, and the applause from the lumber pile could be heard at least two blocks.

After the procession, the entertainment proper consisted of some high and lofty tumbling, the various "turns" of the respective stars, and then, last of all, as a grand finale, Charley, the old raw-boned farm horse who had been retired on a pension for at least a year, was led triumphantly into the ring, with Nickey Burke standing on his back!

Charley, whose melancholy aspect was a trifle more abject than usual, and steps more halting, meekly followed the procession of actors around the ring, led by Dimple, the Snake Charmer. Nickey's entree created a most profound sensation, and was greeted with tumultuous applause—a tribute both to his equestrian feat and to his costume.

Nickey had once attended a circus at which he had been greatly impressed by the artistic decorations on the skin of a tattooed man, and by the skill of the bareback rider who had turned somersaults while the horse was in motion. It occurred to him that perhaps he might present somewhat of both these attractions, in one character.

Maxwell had innocently stimulated this taste by lending him a book illustrated with lurid color-plates of Indians in full war paint, according to tribe.

So Nickey removed his clothes, attired himself in abbreviated red swimming trunks, and submitted to the artistic efforts of Dimple, who painted most intricate, elaborate, and beautiful designs on Nickey's person, with a thick solution of indigo purloined from the laundry.

Nickey's breast was adorned with a picture of a ship under full sail. On his back was a large heart pierced with two arrows. A vine of full blown roses twined around each arm, while his legs were powdered with stars, periods, dashes, and exclamation points in rich profusion. A triangle was painted on each cheek, and dabs of indigo were added to the end of his nose and to the lobe of each ear by way of finishing touches.

When the work was complete, Nickey surveyed himself in a piece of broken mirror in the dressing-room, and to tell the truth, was somewhat appalled at his appearance; but Dimple Perkins hastened to assure him, saying that a dip in the river would easily remove the indigo; and that he was the living spit and image of a tattooed man, and that his appearance, posed on the back of Charley, would certainly bring the house down.

Dimple proved to be quite justified in his statement, so far as the effect on the audience was concerned; for, as Nickey entered the ring, after one moment of breathless astonishment, the entire crowd arose as one man and cheered itself hoarse, in a frenzy of frantic delight. Now whether Charley was enthused by the applause, or whether the situation reminded him of some festive horseplay of his youth, one cannot tell. At any rate, what little life was left in Charley's blood asserted itself. Quickly jerking the rope of the halter from the astonished hand of Dimple Perkins, Charley turned briskly round, and trotted out of the yard and into the road, while Nickey, who had found himself suddenly astride Charley's back, made frantic efforts to stop him.

As Charley emerged from the gate, the freaks, the regular artists, the gymnasts, and the entire audience followed, trailing along behind the mounted tattooed man, and shouting themselves hoarse with encouragement or derision.

As Charley rose to the occasion and quickened his pace, the heat of the sun, the violent exercise of riding bareback, and the nervous excitement produced by the horror of the situation, threw Nickey into a profuse sweat. The bluing began to run. The decorations on his forehead trickled down into his eyes; and as he tried to rub off the moisture with the back of his hand the indigo was smeared liberally over his face. His personal identity was hopelessly obscured in the indigo smudge; and the most vivid imagination could not conjecture what had happened to the boy. It was by no means an easy feat to retain his seat on Charley's back; it would have been still more difficult to dismount, at his steed's brisk pace; and Nickey was most painfully conscious of his attire, as Charley turned up the road which led straight to the village. At each corner the procession was reinforced by a number of village boys who added their quota to the general uproar and varied the monotony of the proceeding by occasionally throwing a tin can at the rider on the white horse. When Charley passed the rectory, and the green, and turned into Church Street, Nickey felt that he had struck rock bottom of shameful humiliation.

For many years it had been Charley's habit to take Mrs. Burke down to church on Wednesday afternoons for the five o'clock service; and although he had been out of commission and docked for repairs for some time, his subliminal self must have got in its work, and the old habit asserted itself: to the church he went, attended at a respectful distance by the Bearded Lady, the Fat Man, the Snake Charmer, the King of the Cannibal Islands, the Living Skeleton, and the Wild Man from Borneo, to say nothing of a large and effective chorus of roaring villagers bringing up the rear.

It really was quite clever of Charley to recall that, this being Wednesday, it was the proper day to visit the church, — as clever as it was disturbing to Nickey when he, too, recalled that it was about time for the service to be over, and that his mother must be somewhere on the premises, to say nothing of the assembled mothers of the entire stock company — and the rector, and the rector's wife.

Mrs. Burke, poor woman, was quite unconscious of what awaited her, as she emerged from the service with the rest of the congregation. It was an amazed parent that caught sight of her son and heir scrambling off the back of his steed onto the horse-block in front of the church, clad in short swimming trunks and much bluing. The freaks, the regular artists, the gymnasts, and the circus audience generally shrieked and howled and fought each other, in frantic effort to succeed to Nickey's place on Charley's back—for Charley now stood undismayed and immovable, with a gentle, pious look in his soft old eyes.

For one instant, Mrs. Burke and her friends stood paralyzed with horror; and then like the good mothers in Israel that they were, each jumped to the rescue of her own particular darling—that is, as soon as she could identify him. Consternation reigned supreme. Mrs. Cooley caught the Bearded Lady by the arm and shook him fiercely, just as he was about to land an uppercut on the jaw of the King of the Cannibal Islands. Mrs. Burns found her offspring, the Fat Man, lying dispossessed on his back in the gutter, while Sime Wilkins, the Man Who Ate Glass, sat comfortably on his stomach. Sime immediately apologized to Mrs. Burns and disappeared. Next, Mrs. Perkins took the Snake Charmer by his collar, and rapped him soundly with the piece of garden hose which she captured as he was using it to chastise the predatory Wild Man from Borneo. Other members of the company received equally unlooked-for censure of their dramatic efforts.

Nickey, meantime, had fled to the pump behind the church, where he made his ablutions as best he could; then, seeing the vestry room door ajar, he, in his extremity, bolted for the quiet seclusion of the sanctuary.

To his surprise and horror, he found Maxwell seated at a table looking over the parish records; and when Nickey appeared, still rather blue, attired in short red trunks, otherwise unadorned, Donald gazed at him in mute astonishment. For one moment there was silence as they eyed each other; and then Maxwell burst into roars of uncontrollable laughter, which were not quite subdued as Nickey gave a rather incoherent account of the misfortune which had brought him to such a predicament.

"So you were the Tattooed Man, were you! Well, I suppose you know that it's not generally customary to appear in church in red tights; but as you couldn't help it, I shall have to see what can be done for you, to get you home clothed and in your right mind. I'll tell you! You can put on one of the choir boy's cassocks, and skip home the back way. If anybody stops you tell them you were practising for the choir, and it will be all right. But really, Nickey, if I were in your place, the next time I posed as a mounted Tattooed Man, I'd be careful to choose some old quadruped that couldn't run away with you!"

"Then you aren't mad at me!"

"Certainly not. I'll leave that to my betters! You just get home as fast as you can."

"Gee! but you're white all right—you know it didn't say nothing in the book, about what kind of paint to use!"

Maxwell's eyes opened. "What book are you talking about, Nickey?" he asked.

"The one you let me take, with the Indians in it."

Maxwell had to laugh again. "So that's where the idea for this 'Carnival of Wild West Sports' originated, eh?"

"Yes, sir," Nickey nodded. "Everybody wanted to be the tattooed man, but seeing as I had the book, and old Charley was my horse, I couldn't see any good reason why I shouldn't get tattooed. Gee! I'll bet ma will be mad!"

After being properly vested in a cassock two sizes too large for him, Nickey started on a dead run for home, and, having reached the barn, dressed himself in his customary attire. When he appeared at supper Mrs. Burke did not say anything; but after the dishes were washed she took him apart and listened to his version of the affair.

"Nicholas Burke," she said, "if this thing occurs again I shall punish you in a way you won't like."

"Well, I'm awfully sorry," said Nickey, "but it didn't seem to feaze Mr. Maxwell a little bit. He just sat and roared as if he'd split his sides. I guess I 'aint goin' to be put out of the church just yet, anyway."

Mrs. Burke looked a bit annoyed.

"Never mind about Mr. Maxwell. *You* won't laugh if anything like this occurs again, I can tell you," she replied.

"Now, ma," soothed Nickey, "don't you worry about it occurrin' again. You don't suppose I did it on purpose, do you? Gosh no! I wouldn't get onto Charley's back again, with my clothes off, any more than I'd sit on a hornet's nest. How'd you like to ride through the town with nothin' on but your swimmin' trunks and drippin' with bluin water, I'd like to know?"

Mrs. Burke did not care to prolong the interview any further, so she said in her severest tones:

"Nicholas Burke, you go to bed instantly. I've heard enough of you and seen enough of you, for one day."

Nickey went.

CHAPTER XIV

ON THE SIDE PORCH

In the evening, after his work was done, a day or two after his talk with Mrs. Maxwell, Jonathan went into the house and took a long look at himself in the glass, with the satisfactory conclusion that he didn't look so old after all. Why shouldn't he take Mrs. Betty's advice and marry? To be sure, there was no fool like an old fool, but no man could be called a fool who was discriminating enough, and resourceful enough, to win the hand of Hepsey Burke. To his certain knowledge she had had plenty of eligible suitors since her husband's death. She was the acknowledged past-master of doughnuts; and her pickled cucumbers done in salad oil were dreams of delight. What more could a man want?

So he found that the question was deciding itself apparently without any volition whatever on his part. His fate was sealed; he had lost his heart and his appetite to his neighbor. Having come to this conclusion, it was wonderful how the thought excited him. He took a bath and changed his clothes, and then proceeded to town and bought himself a white neck-tie, and a scarf-pin that cost seventy-five cents. He was going to do the thing in the proper way if he did it at all.

After supper he mustered sufficient courage to present himself at the side porch where Mrs. Burke was knitting on a scarlet sweater for Nickey.

"Good evenin', Hepsey," he began. "How are you feelin' to-night?"

"Oh, not so frisky as I might, Jonathan; I'd be all right if it weren't for my rheumatiz."

"Well, we all have our troubles, Hepsey; and if it isn't one thing it's most generally another. You mustn't rebel against rheumatiz. It's one of those things sent to make us better, and we must bear up against it, you know."

Hepsey did not respond to this philosophy, and Jonathan felt that it was high time that he got down to business. So he began again:

"It seems to me as if we might have rain before long if the wind don't change."

"Shouldn't be surprised, Jonathan. One—two—three—four—" Mrs. Burke replied, her attention divided between her visitor and her sweater. "Got your hay all in?"

"Yes, most of it. 'Twon't be long before the long fall evenin's will be comin' on, and I kinder dread 'em. They're awful lonesome, Hepsey."

"Purl two, knit two, an inch and a half—" Mrs. Burke muttered to herself as she read the printed directions which lay in her lap, and then she added encouragingly:

"So you get lonesome, do you, Jonathan, durin' the long evenin's, when it gets dark early."

"Oh, awful lonesome," Jonathan responded. "Don't you ever get lonesome yourself, Hepsey?"

"I can't say as it kept me awake nights. 'Tisn't bein' alone that makes you lonesome. The most awful lonesomeness in the world is bein' in a crowd that's not your kind."

"That's so, Hepsey. But two isn't a crowd. Don't you think you'd like to get married, if you had a right good chance, now?"

Hepsey gave her visitor a quick, sharp glance, and inquired:

"What would you consider a right good chance, Jonathan?"

"Oh, suppose that some respectable widower with a tidy sum in the bank should ask you to marry him; what would you say, Hepsey?"

"Can't say until I'd seen the widower, to say nothin' of the bank book—one, two, three, four, five, six—"

Jonathan felt that the crisis was now approaching; so, moving his chair a little nearer, he resumed excitedly:

"You've seen him, Hepsey; you've seen him lots of times, and he don't live a thousand miles away, neither."

"Hm! Must be he lives in Martin's Junction. Is he good lookin', Jonathan?"

"Oh, fair to middlin'. That is—of course—I well—I—I should think he was; but tastes differ."

"Well, you know I'm right particular, Jonathan. Is he real smart and clever?"

"I don't know as—I ought to—to—say, Hepsey; but I rather guess he knows enough to go in when it rains."

"That's good as far as it goes. The next time you see him, you tell him to call around and let me look him over. Maybe I could give him a job on the farm, even if I didn't want to marry him."

"But he doesn't want any job on the farm, Hepsey. He just wants you, that's all."

"How do you know he does? Did he ever tell you?"

"Hepsey Burke, don't you know who I'm alludin' at? Haven't you ever suspected nothin'?"

"Yes, I've suspected lots of things. Now there's Jack Dempsey. I've suspected him waterin' the milk for some time. Haven't you ever suspected anythin' yourself, Jonathan?"

"Well, I guess I'm suspectin' that you're tryin' to make a fool of me, all right."

"Oh no! Fools come ready-made, and there's a glut in the market just now; seven—eight—nine—ten; no use makin' more until the supply's exhausted. But what made you think you wanted to marry? This is so powerful sudden."

Now that the point was reached, Jonathan got a little nervous: "To—to tell you the truth, Hepsey," he stuttered, "I was in doubt about it myself for some time; but bein' as I am a Christian man I turned to the Bible for light on my path."

"Hm! And how did the light shine?"

"Well, I just shut my eyes and opened my Bible at random, and put my finger on a text. Then I opened my eyes and read what was written."

"Yes! What did you find?"

"I read somethin' about 'not a man of them escaped save six hundred that rode away on camels.'"

"Did that clear up all your difficulties?"

"No, can't say as it did. But those words about 'no man escapin'' seemed to point towards matrimony as far as they went. Then I tried a second time."

"Oh did you? I should think that six hundred camels would be enough for one round-up. What luck did you have the second time?"

"Well, I read, 'Moab is my wash pot, over Edom will I cast out my shoe.' You've seen 'em cast shoes at the carriages of brides and grooms, haven't you, Hepsey? Just for luck, you know. So it seemed to point towards matrimony again."

"Say, Jonathan, you certainly have a wonderful gift for interpretin' Scripture."

"Well, Scripture or no Scripture, I want you, Hepsey."

"Am I to understand that you're just fadin' and pinin' away for love of me? You don't look thin."

"Oh, we 'aint neither of us as young as we once was, Hepsey. Of course I can't be expected to pine real hard."

"I'm afraid it's not the real thing, Jonathan, unless you pine. Don't it keep you awake nights, or take away your appetite, or make you want to play the banjo, or nothin'?"

"No, Hepsey; to tell you the plain truth, it don't. But I feel awful lonesome, and I like you a whole lot, and I—I love you as much as anyone, I guess."

"So you are in love are you, Jonathan. Then let me give you some good advice. When you're in love, don't believe all you think, or half you feel, or anything at all you are perfectly sure of. It's dangerous business. But I am afraid that you're askin' me because it makes you think that you are young and giddy, like the rest of the village boys, to be proposin' to a shy young thing like me."

"No, Hepsey; you aren't no shy young thing, and you haven't been for nigh on forty years. I wouldn't be proposin' to you if you were."

"Jonathan, your manners need mendin' a whole lot. The idea of insinuatin' that I am not a shy young thing. I'm ashamed of you, and I'm positive we could never get along together."

"But I can't tell a lie about you, even if I do want to marry you. You don't want to marry a liar, do you?"

"Well, the fact is, Jonathan, polite lyin's the real foundation of all good manners. What we'll ever do when we get to heaven where we have to tell the truth whether we want to or not, I'm sure I don't know. It'll be awful uncomfortable until we get used to it."

"The law says you should tell the truth, the whole truth, and nothin' but the truth," persisted the literal wooer.

"Now, see here, Jonathan. Would you say that a dog's tail was false and misleadin' just because it isn't the whole dog?"

This proposition was exceedingly confusing to Jonathan's intelligence, but after careful consideration he felt obliged to say "No."

"Of course you wouldn't," Mrs. Burke continued triumphantly, quickly following up her advantage. "You see a dog's tail couldn't be misleading, 'cause the dog leads the tail, and not the tail the dog. Any fool could see that."

Jonathan felt that he had been tricked, although he could not see just how the thing had been accomplished; so he began again:

"Now Hepsey, we're wanderin' from the point, and you're just talkin' to amuse yourself. Can't you come down to business? Here I am a widower, and here you are a widowess, and we're both lonesome, and we—"

"Who told you I was lonesome, I'd like to know?"

"Well, of course you didn't, 'cause you never tell anything to anyone. But I guessed you was sometimes, from the looks of you."

Hepsey bent her head over her work and counted stitches a long time before she looked up. Then she remarked slowly:

"There's an awful lot of sick people in the world, and I'm mighty sorry for 'em; but they'll die, or they'll get well. I guess I'm more sorry for people who have to go on livin', and workin' hard, when they're just dyin' for somebody to love 'em, and somebody to love, until the pain of it hurts like a wisdom tooth. No, I can't afford to be lonesome much, and that's a fact. So I just keep busy, and if I get too lonesome, I just go and jolly somebody that's lonesomer than I am, and we both feel better; and if I get lonely lyin' awake at night, I light a lamp and read Webster's Dictionary. Try it, Jonathan; it's a sure anti-doubt."

"There you go again, tryin' to change the subject, just when I thought you was goin' to say somethin'."

"But you don't really want to marry me. I'm not young, and I'm not interestin': one or the other you've just got to be."

"You're mighty interestin' to me, Hepsey, anyway; and—and you're mighty unselfish."

"Well, you needn't throw that in my face; I'm not to blame for bein' unselfish. I've just had to be, whether I wanted or not. It's my misfortune, not my fault. Lots of people are unselfish because they're too weak to stand up for their own rights." She paused—and then looked up at him, smiling whimsically, and added: "Well, well, Jonathan; see here now—I'll think it over, and perhaps some day before—*go 'way*, you horrid thing! Let go my hand, I tell you. There! You've made me drop a whole row of stitches. If you don't run over home right now, before you're tempted to do any more flirtin, I'll— I'll hold you for breach of promise."

CHAPTER XV

NICKEY'S SOCIAL AMBITIONS

To Nickey, the Maxwells were in the nature of a revelation. At his impressionable stage of boyhood, and because of their freedom from airs and graces of any kind, he was quick to notice the difference in type—"some class to them; not snobs or dudes, but the real thing," as he expressed it. His ardent admiration of Donald, and his adoration of Mrs. Betty, gave him ambition to find the key to their secret, and to partake of it.

He was too shy to speak of it,—to his mother last of all, as is the nature of a boy,—and had to rely on an observant and receptive mind for the earlier steps in his quest. When Maxwell boarded with them, Nickey had discovered that he was won't to exercise with dumb-bells each morning before breakfast. The very keenness of his desire to be initiated, held him silent. A visit to the town library, on his mother's behalf, chanced to bring his eyes—generally oblivious of everything in the shape of a book—upon the title of a certain volume designed to instruct in various parlor-feats of physical prowess.

The book was borrowed from the librarian,—a little shamefacedly. The next morning Mrs. Burke was somewhat alarmed at the noise which came from Nickey's room, and when there was a crash as if the chimney had fallen, she could stand it no longer, and hurried aloft. Nickey stood in the middle of the floor, clad in swimming trunks, gripping a large weight (purloined from the barn) in either hand, very red in the face, and much out of breath.

As the door unexpectedly opened he dived for bed and pulled the clothes under his chin.

"Land Sakes!" Hepsey breathed, aghast. "What's all this about? If there's a nail loose in the flooring I can lend you a hammer for the asking," and she examined several jagged dents in the boards.

"Say ma," urged Nickey in moving tones. "If I'd a pair of dumb-bells like Mr. Maxwell's, I c'd hold onto 'em. I've pretty near smashed my feet with them things—gosh darn it," he added ruefully, nursing the bruised member under the clothes.

"I guess you can get 'em, next time you go to Martin's Junction; but if it's exercise you want," his parent remarked unsympathetically, "there's plenty of kindlin' in the woodshed wants choppin'."

She retired chuckling to herself, as she caught a glimmer of what was working in her son's mind.

The "reading habit" having been inculcated by this lucky find at the library, it was not long before Nickey acquired from the same source a veritable collection of volumes on the polite arts and crafts—"The Ready Letter-Writer"; "Manners Maketh Man"; "Seven Thousand Errors of Speech;" "Social Culture in the Smart Set," and the like.

Nickey laboriously studied from these authorities how to enter a ball room, how to respond to a toast at a dinner given in one's honor, how to propose the health of his hostess, and how to apologize for treading on a lady's train.

In the secrecy of his chamber he put into practice the helpful suggestions of these invaluable manuals. He bowed to the washstand, begged the favor of the next dance from the towel rack, trod on the window shade and made the prescribed apology. Then he discussed the latest novel at dinner with a distinguished personage; and having smoked an invisible cigar, interspersed with such wit as accords with walnuts and wine, after the ladies had retired, he entered the drawing-room, exchanged parting amenities with the guests, bade his hostess good night, and gracefully withdrew to the clothes-press.

Several times Hepsey caught glimpses of him going through the dumb show of "Social Culture in the Smart Set," and her wondering soul was filled with astonishment at his amazing evolutions. She found it in her heart to speak of it to Mrs. Betty and Maxwell, and ask for their interpretation of the matter.

So, one day, during this seizure of feverish enthusiasm for self-culture, Hepsey and Nickey received an invitation to take supper at the rectory. Nevertheless, Mrs. Burke thought it prudent to give her son some good advice in regard to his behavior. She realized, perhaps, that a book is good so far as it goes, but is apt to ignore elementals. So she called him aside before they started:

"Now, Nickey, remember to act like a gentleman, especially at the table; you must try to do credit to your bringin' up."

"Yes, I'll do my level best if it kills me," the boy replied.

"Well, what do you do with your napkin when you first sit down to the table?"

"Tie it 'round my neck, of course!"

"Oh, no, you mustn't do anything of the sort; you must just tuck it in your collar, like any gentleman would. And when we come home what are you goin' to say to Mrs. Maxwell?"

"Oh, I'll say, 'I'll see you later.'"

"Mercy no! Say, 'I've had a very nice time.'"

"But suppose I didn't have a nice time,—what'd I say?"

For a moment Hepsey struggled to reconcile her code of ethics with her idea of good manners, and then replied:

"Why say, 'Mrs. Maxwell, it was awfully good of you to ask me,' and I don't believe she'll notice anything wrong about that."

"Hm!" Nickey retorted scornfully. "Seems pretty much like the same thing to me."

"Oh no! Not in the least. Now what will you wear when we go to the rectory?"

"My gray suit, and tan shoes, and the green tie with the purple spots on it."

"Who'll be the first to sit down to the table?"

"Search me—maybe I will, if there's good eats."

"Nonsense! You must wait for Mrs. Maxwell and the rector to be seated first."

"Well," Nickey exclaimed in exasperation, "I'm bound to make some horrible break anyway, so don't you worry, ma. It seems to me from what them books say, that when you go visitin' you've got to tell lies like a sinner; and you can't tell the truth till you get home with the door shut. I never was good at lyin'; I always get caught."

"It isn't exactly lyin', Nickey; its just sayin' nice things, and keepin' your mouth shut about the rest. Now suppose you dropped a fork under the table, what'd you say?"

"I'd say ''scuse me, Mrs. Maxwell, but one of the forks has gone, and you can go through my clothes if you want to before I go home.'"

"Hm!" Hepsey remarked dryly, "I guess the less you say, the better."

Arrived at the rectory, Nickey felt under some restraint when they first sat down to the supper table; but under the genial manner of Mrs. Maxwell he soon felt at his ease, and not even his observant mother detected any dire breach of table etiquette. His conversation was somewhat spare, his attention being absorbed and equally divided between observation of his host and consumption of the feast set before him. With sure tact, Mrs. Betty—though regarding Nickey as the guest of honor—that evening—deferred testing the results of his conversational studies until after supper: one thing at once, she decided, was fair play.

After the meal was over, they repaired together to the parlor, and while Hepsey took out her wash-rag knitting and Maxwell smoked his cigar, Mrs. Betty gave Nickey her undivided attention.

In order to interest the young people of the place in the missionary work of the parish, Mrs. Betty had organized a guild of boys who were to earn what they could towards the support of a missionary in the west. The Guild had been placed under the fostering care and supervision of Nickey as its treasurer, and was known by the name of "The Juvenile Band of Gleaners." In the course of the evening Mrs. Maxwell took occasion to inquire what progress they were making, thereby unconsciously challenging a somewhat surprising recountal.

"Well," Nickey replied readily, "we've got forty-six cents in the treasury; that's just me, you know; I keep the cash in my pants pocket."

Then he smiled uneasily, and fidgeted in his chair.

There was something in Nickey's tone and look that excited Mrs. Betty's curiosity, and made his mother stop knitting and look at him anxiously over her glasses.

"That is very good for a start," Mrs. Betty commended. "How did you raise all that, Nickey?"

For a moment Nickey colored hotly, looked embarrassed, and made no reply. Then mustering up his courage, and laughing, he began:

"Well, Mrs. Maxwell, it was just like this. Maybe you won't like it, but I'll tell you all the same. Bein' as I was the president of the Juv'nul Band of Gleaners, I though I'd get the kids together, and start somethin'. Saturday it rained cats and dogs, so Billy Burns, Sam Cooley, Dimple Perkins and me, we went up into the hay loft, and I said to the kids, 'You fellows have got to cough up some dough for the church, and—'"

"Contribute money, Nickey. Don't be slangy," his mother interjected.

"Well I says, 'I'm runnin' the Juv'nals, and you've got to do just what I say. I've got a dandy scheme for raisin' money and we'll have some fun doin' it, or I miss my guess.' Then I asked Sam Cooley how much money he'd got, and Sam, he had forty-four cents, Billy Burns had fifty-two cents, and Dimple had only two. Dimp never did have much loose cash, anyway. But I said to Dimp, 'Never mind, Dimp; you aint to blame. Your dad's an old skinflint. I'll lend you six to start off with.' Then I made Billy Burns sweep the floor, while Sam went down to the chicken yard and caught my bantam rooster, Tooley. Then I sent Dimp after some chalk, and an empty peach basket, and a piece of cord. Then we was ready for business.

"I marked a big circle on the barn floor with the chalk, and divided it into four quarters with straight lines runnin' through the middle. Then I turned the peach basket upside down, and tied one end of the string on the bottom, and threw the other end up over a beam overhead, so I could pull the basket off from the floor up to the beam by the string. You see," Nickey illustrated with graphic gestures, "the basket hung just over the middle of the circle like a bell. Then I took the rooster and stuck him under the basket. Tooley hollered and scratched like Sam Hill and—"

"For mercy sake, Nickey! What will you say next?"

"Say, ma, you just wait and see. Well, Tooley kicked like everything, but he had to go under just the same. Then I said to the kids to sit around the circle on the floor, and each choose one of the four quarters for hisself,—one for each of us. 'Now,' I said, 'you must each cough up—'"

"Nicholas!"

"Oh ma, do let me tell it without callin' me down every time. 'You kids must hand out a cent apiece and put it on the floor in your own quarter. Then, when I say ready, I'll pull the string and raise the basket and let Tooley out. Tooley'll get scared and run. If he runs off the circle through my quarter, then the four cents are mine; but if he runs through Dimp's quarter, then the four cents are Dimp's.'

"It was real excitin' when I pulled the string, and the basket went up. You'd ought to 've been there, Mrs. Maxwell. You'd have laughed fit to split—"

"Nicholas Burke, you must stop talkin' like that, or I'll send you home," reproved Mrs. Burke, looking severely at her son, and with deprecating side-glances at his audience.

"Excuse me, ma. It will be all over in a minute. But really, you'd have laughed like sin—I mean you'd have just laughed yourself sick. Tooley was awful nervous when the basket went up. For a minute he crouched and stood still, scared stiff at the three kids, all yellin' like mad; then he ducked his head and bolted off the circle through my quarter and flew up on a beam. I thought the kids would bust."

Mrs. Burke sighed heavily.

"Well, burst, then. But while they were laughin' I raked in the cash. You see I just had to. I won it for fair. I'd kept quiet, and that's why Tooley come across my quarter."

Mrs. Maxwell was sorting over her music, while Maxwell's face was hidden behind a paper. Mrs. Burke was silent through despair. Nickey glanced furtively at his hearers for a moment and then continued:

"Yes, the kids was tickled; but they got awful quiet when I told them to fork over another cent apiece for the jack-pot."

"What in the name of conscience is a jack-pot?" Hepsey asked.

Donald laughed and Nickey continued:

"A jack-pot's a jack-pot; there isn't no other name that I ever heard of. We caught Tooley and stuck him under the basket, and made him do it all over again. You see, every time when Tooley got loose, the kids all leant forward and yelled like mad; but I just kept my mouth shut, and leaned way back out of the way so that Tooley'd run out through my quarter. So I won most all the time."

There was a pause, while Nickey looked a bit apprehensively at his audience. But he went on gamely to the end of the chapter.

"Once Tooley made a bolt in a straight line through Dimp's quarter, and hit Dimp in the mouth, and bowled him over like a nine-pin. Dimp was scared to death, and howled like murder till he found

111

he'd scooped the pot; then he got quiet. After we made Tooley run ten times, he struck work and wouldn't run any more; so we just had to let him go; but I didn't care nothn' about that, 'cause you see I had the kids' cash in my pants pocket, and that was what I was after. Well, sir, when it was all over, 'cause I'd busted the bank—"

"Nicholas Burke, I am ashamed of you."

"Never mind, ma; I'm most through now. When they found I'd busted the bank, they looked kind of blue, and Dimp Perkins said it was a skin game, and I was a bunco steerer."

"What did you say to that?" Donald inquired.

"Oh, I just said it was all for religion, it was church money, and it was all right. I was just gleanin' what few cents they had, to pay the church debt to the missionary; and they ought to be ashamed to have a church debt hangin' over 'em, and they'd oughter be more cheerful 'bout givin' a little somethin' toward raisin' of it."

When Nickey had finished, there was an ominous silence for a moment or two, and then his mother said sternly:

"What do you suppose Mrs. Perkins will say when she finds that you've tricked her son into a regular gambling scheme, to get his money away from him?"

"Mrs. Perkins," retorted Nickey, thoroughly aroused by the soft impeachment. "I should worry! At the church fair, before Mr. Maxwell came, she ran a fancy table, and tried to sell a baby blanket to an old bachelor; but he wouldn't take it. Then when he wasn't lookin', blessed if she didn't turn around and tie the four corners together with a bit of ribbon, and sell it to him for a handkerchief case. She got two dollars for it, and it wasn't worth seventy-five cents. She was as proud as a dog with two tails, and went around tellin' everybody."

Silence reigned, ominous and general, and Nickey braced himself for the storm. Even Mrs. Maxwell didn't look at him, and that was pretty bad. He began to get hot all over, and the matter was fast assuming a new aspect in his own mind which made him ashamed of himself. His spirits sank lower and lower. Finally his mother remarked quietly:

"Nickey, I thought you were goin' to be a gentleman."

"That's straight, all right, what I've told you," he murmured abashed.

There was another silent pause—presently broken by Nickey.

"I guess I hadn't thought about it, just that way. I guess I'll give the kids their money back," he volunteered despondently—"only I'll have to make it up, some way, in the treasury." He felt in his pockets, and jingled the coins.

Another pause—with only the ticking of his mother's knitting needles to relieve the oppressive silence. Suddenly the worried pucker disappeared from his brow, and his face brightened like a sun-burst.

"I've got it, Mrs. Maxwell," he cried. "I've got seventy-five cents comin' to me down at the Variety Store, for birch-bark frames, and I'll give that for the blamed old missionaries. That's square, 'aint it now?"

Mrs. Betty's commendation and her smile were salve to the wounds of her young guest, and Donald's hearty laughter soon dispelled the sense of social failure which was beginning to cloud Nickey's happy spirit.

"Say Nickey," said Maxwell, throwing down his paper, "Mrs. Betty and I want to start a Boy Scout Corps in the parish, and with your resourceful genius you could get the boys together, and explain it to them, and soon we should have the whole thing in ship-shape order. Will you do it?"

"Will I?" exclaimed the delighted recruit. "I guess so—but some of 'em 'aint 'Piscopals, Mr. Maxwell; there's Sam Cooley, he's a Methodist, and—"

"That doesn't cut any ice, Nickey,—excuse my slang, ladies," he apologized to his wife and Hepsey, at which the boy grinned with delight. "We're out to welcome all comers. I've got the books that we shall need upstairs. Let's go up to my den and talk it all over. We shall have to spend evenings getting thoroughly up in it ourselves, — rules and knots and first-aid and the rest. Mrs. Burke will allay parental anxiety as to the bodily welfare of the recruits and the pacific object of the organization, and Mrs. Maxwell will make the colors. Come on!"

With sparkling eyes, Nickey followed Donald out of the room; as they disappeared Hepsey slowly shook her head in grateful deprecation at Betty.

"Bless him!" ejaculated Hepsey. "Mixin' up religion, with a little wholesome fun, is the only way you can serve it to boys, like Nickey, and get results. Boys that are ever goin' to amount to anything are too full of life to stand 'em up in a row, with a prayer book in one hand and a hymnal in the other, and expect 'em to sprout wings. It can't be done. Keep a boy outside enough and he'll turn out alright. Fresh air and open fields have a mighty helpful influence on 'em. The way I've got it figgered out, all of us can absorb a lot of the right kind of religion, if we'll only go out and watch old Mother Nature, now and then."

CHAPTER XVI
PRACTICAL
TEMPERANCE
REFORM

The small town of Durford was not immune from the curse of drink: there was no doubt about that. Other forms of viciousness there were in plenty; but the nine saloons did more harm than all the rest of the evil influences put together, and Maxwell, though far from being a fanatic, was doing much in a quiet way to neutralize their bad influence. He turned the Sunday School room into a reading room during the week days, organized a gymnasium, kept watch of the younger men individually, and offered as best he could some chance for the expression of the gregarious instinct which drew them together after the work of the day was over. In the face of his work in these directions, it happened that a venturesome and enterprising saloon-keeper bought a vacant property adjacent to the church, and opened up an aggressive business — much to Maxwell's dismay.

Among the women of the parish there was a "Ladies' Temperance League," of which Mrs. Burke was president. They held quarterly meetings, and it was at one of the meetings held at Thunder Cliff, and at which Mrs. Burke presided, that she remarked severely:

"Mrs. Sapley, you're out of order. There's a motion before the house, and I've got something to say about it myself. Mrs. Perkins, as Mrs. Maxwell was unable to be present, will you kindly take the chair, or anything else you can lay your hands on, and I'll say what I've got to say."

Mrs. Perkins took Mrs. Burke's place as the president, while Mrs. Burke rubbed her glasses in an impatient way; and having adjusted them, began in a decided tone from which there was meant to be no appeal:

"The fact is, ladies, we're not gettin' down to business as we ought to, if we are to accomplish anything. We've been singing hymns, and recitin' lovely poems, and listenin' to reports as to how money spent for liquor would pay off the national debt; and we've been sayin' prayers, and pledgin' ourselves not to do things none of us ever was tempted to do, or thought of doin', and wearin' ribbons, and attendin' conventions, and talkin' about influencin' legislation at Washington, and eatin' sandwiches, and drinkin' weak tea, and doin' goodness knows what; but we've not done a blessed thing to stop men drinkin' right here in Durford and breakin' the town law; you know that well enough."

Mrs. Burke paused for breath after this astounding revolutionary statement, and there was a murmur of scandalized dissent from the assembled ladies at this outspoken expression on the part of the honorable president of the Parish Guild.

"No," she continued emphatically, "don't you fool yourselves. If we can't help matters right here where we live, then there's no use havin' imitation church sociables, and goin' home thinkin' we've helped the temperance cause, and callin' everybody else bad names who don't exactly agree with us."

Again there were symptoms of open rebellion against this traitorous heresy on the part of the plainspoken president; but she was not to be easily silenced; so she continued:

"Men have got to go somewheres when their work is over, and have a good time, and I believe that we won't accomplish anything until we fix up a nice, attractive set of rooms with games, and give 'em something to drink."

Cries of "Oh! Oh! Oh!" filled the room.

"I didn't say whiskey, did I? Anybody would think I'd offered to treat you, the way you receive my remarks. Now we can't get the rooms right off, 'cause we can't yet afford to pay the rent of 'em. But there's one thing we can do. There's Silas Bingham—the new man. He's gone and opened a saloon within about a hundred feet of the church, and he's sellin' liquor to children and runnin' a slot machine besides. It's all against the law; but if you think the village trustees are goin' to do anythin' to enforce the law, you're just dead wrong, every one of you. The trustees are most of 'em in it for graft, and they 'aint goin' to close no saloon when it's comin' election day 'for long, not if Bingham serves cocktails between the hymns in church. Maybe the trustees'd come to church better if he did. Maybe you think I'm usin' strong language; but it's true all the same, and you know it's true. Silas Bingham's move is a sassy challenge to us: are we goin' to lie down under it?"

"I must say that I'm painfully surprised at you, Mrs. Burke," Mrs. Burns began. "You surely can't forget what wonderful things the League has accomplished in Virginia and—"

"Yes," Mrs. Burke interrupted, "but you see Durford 'aint in Virginia so far as heard from, and it's our business to get up and hustle right here where we live. Did you think we were tryin' to reform Virginia or Alaska by absent treatment?"

Mrs. Sapley could not contain herself another moment; so, rising to her feet excitedly she sputtered:

"I do not agree with you, Mrs. Burke; I do not agree with you at all. Our meetings have been very inspiring and helpful to us all, I am perfectly sure; very uplifting and encouraging; and I am astonished that you should speak as you do."

"I'm very glad you've found them so, Mrs. Sapley. I don't drink myself, and I don't need no encouragin' and upliftin'. It's the weak man that drinks who needs encouragin' and upliftin'; and he wouldn't come near one of our meetin's any more than a bantam rooster would try to hatch turtles from moth-balls. We've got to clear Silas Bingham from off the church steps."

"Well," Mrs. Burns inquired, "what do you propose to do about it, if I may be allowed to inquire?"

"Do? The first thing I propose to do is to interview Silas Bingham myself privately, and see what I can do with him. Perhaps I won't accomplish nothin'; but I'm goin' to try, anyway, and make him get out of that location."

"You can, if anybody can," Mrs. Sapley remarked.

"Thank you for the compliment, Mrs. Sapley. Now Mrs. President, I move, sir—that is, madam—that the parish League appoints me to interview Bingham."

The motion was duly seconded and passed, notwithstanding some mild protests from the opposition, and Mrs. Burke resumed her place as presiding officer of the meeting. Then she continued:

"Excuse me; I forgot the previous question which somebody moved. Shall we have lettuce or chicken sandwiches at our next meetin'? You have heard the question. Those in favor of chicken please say aye. Ah! The ayes have the chicken, and the chicken is unanimously carried. Any more business to come before the meetin'? If not, we'll proceed to carry out the lit'ary program arranged by Miss Perkins. Then we'll close this meetin' by singin' the 224th hymn. Don't forget the basket by the door."

Silas Bingham was an undersized, timid, pulpy soul, with a horizontal forehead, watery blue eyes, and a receding chin. Out of "office hours" he looked like a meek solicitor for a Sunday School magazine. One bright morning just as he had finished sweeping out the saloon and was polishing the brass rod on the front of the bar, Mrs. Burke walked in, and extended her hand to the astonished bar-keeper, whose chin dropped from sheer amazement. She introduced herself in the most cordial and sympathetic of tones, saying:

"How do you do, Mr. Bingham? I haven't had the pleasure of meetin' you before; but I always make it a point to call on strangers when they come to town. It must be awful lonesome when you first arrive and don't know a livin' soul. I hope your wife is tolerable well."

Bingham gradually pulled himself together and turned very red, as he replied:

"Thanks! But my wife doesn't live here. It's awful kind of you, I'm sure; but you'll find my wife in the third house beyond the bakery, down two blocks—turn to the right. She'll be glad to see you."

"That's good," Hepsey responded, "but you see I don't have much to do on Thursdays, and I'll just have a little visit with you, now I'm here. Fine day, isn't it."

Mrs. Burke drew up a chair and sat down, adjusted her feet comfortably to the rung of another chair, and pulled out her knitting from her work-bag, much to the consternation of the proprietor of the place.

"How nice you've got things fixed up, Mr. Bingham," Hepsey remarked, gazing serenely at the seductive variety of bottles and glasses, and the glare of mirrors behind the bar. "Nothin' like havin' a fine lookin' place to draw trade. Is business prosperin' now-a-days?"

Silas turned three shades redder, and stammered badly as he replied:

"Yes, I'm doin' as well as I can expect—er—I suppose."

"Probably as well as your customers are doin', I should imagine? You don't need to get discouraged. It takes time to work up a trade like yours in a nice, decent neighborhood like this."

Silas stared hard at the unwelcome intruder, glancing apprehensively at the door from which several customers had already turned away when, through the glass, they had caught sight of Mrs. Burke. He was desperately ill at ease, and far from responding cordially to Hepsey's friendly advances; and his nervousness increased as his patrons continually retreated, occasionally grinning derisively at him through the glass in the door.

"If you don't mind my sayin' it, Mrs. Burke, I think you'd be a lot more comfortable at my house than you are here."

"Oh, I'm perfectly comfortable, thanks; perfectly comfortable. Don't you worry a bit about me."

"But this is a saloon, and it 'aint just what you might call respectable for ladies to be sittin' in a saloon, now, is it?"

"Why not?"

The question was so sudden, sharp and unexpected that Silas jumped and almost knocked over a bottle of gin, and then stared in silent chagrin at his guest, his nervous lips moving without speech.

"I don't see," Hepsey continued, "just why the men should have all the fun, and then when a woman takes to enjoyin' herself say that it isn't respectable. What's the difference, I'd like to know? This is a right cheerful place, and I feel just like stayin' as long as I want to. There's no law against a woman goin' to a saloon, is there? I saw Jane Dwire come out of here Saturday night. To be sure, Jane 'aint just what you'd call a 'society' lady, as you might say; but as long as I behave myself I don't see why I should go."

"But, ma'am," Silas protested in wrathful desperation, "I must ask you to go. You'll hurt my trade if you stay here any longer."

"Hurt your trade! Nonsense! You aren't half as polite as I thought you were. I'm awful popular with the gentlemen. You ought to be payin' me a commission to sit here and entertain your customers, instead of insinuatin' that I 'aint welcome. Ah! Here comes Martin Crowfoot. Haven't seen Martin in the longest time."

Martin slouched in and reached the bar and ordered before he caught sight of Mrs. Burke. He was just raising the glass to his lips when Hepsey stepped up briskly, and extending her hand, exclaimed:

"How do you do, Martin? How are the folks at home? Awful glad to see you."

Martin stared vacantly at Mrs. Burke, dropped his glass, and muttered incoherently. Then he bolted hastily from the place without paying for his drink.

Bingham was now getting a bit hysterical over the situation, and was about to make another vigorous protest, when Hiram Green entered and called for some beer. Again Hepsey extended her hand cordially, and Hiram jumped as if he had seen a ghost—for they had been friendly for years.

"Hepsey Burke, what in the name of all that's decent are you doin' in a place like this?" he demanded when he could get his breath. "Don't you know you'll ruin your reputation if you're seen sittin' in a saloon?"

"Oh, don't let that worry you, Hiram, My reputation'd freeze a stroke of lightnin'. You don't seem to be worryin' much about your own reputation."

"Oh well, a man can do a lot of things a woman can't, without losin' his reputation."

For an instant the color flamed into Mrs. Burke's face as she retorted hotly:

"Yes, there's the whole business. A man can drink, and knock the seventh commandment into a cocked hat; and then when he wants to settle down and get married he demands a wife as white as snow. If he gets drunk, it's a lark. If she gets drunk, it's a crime. But I didn't come here to preach or hold a revival, and as for my welfare and my reputation, Mr. Bingham and I was just havin' a pleasant afternoon together when you came in and interrupted us. He's awful nice when you get to know him real intimate. Now, Hiram, I hate to spoil your fun, and you do look a bit thirsty. Suppose you have a lemonade on me, if you're sure it won't go to your head. It isn't often that we get out like this together. Lemonades for two, Mr. Bingham; and make Hiram's real sweet."

Mrs. Burke enjoyed hugely the disgust and the grimaces with which Green swallowed the syrupy mixture. He then beat a hasty retreat down the street. For two hours Hepsey received all who were courageous enough to venture in, with most engaging smiles and cordial handshakes, until Silas was bordering on madness. Finally he emerged from the bar and mustered up sufficient courage to threaten:

"Mrs. Burke, if you don't quit, I'll send for the police," he blustered.

Hepsey gazed calmly at her victim and replied:

"I wouldn't, if I was in your place."

"Well then, I give you fair warning I'll put you out myself if you don't go peaceable in five minutes."

"No, Silas; you're wrong as usual. You can't put me out of here until I'm ready to go. I could wring you out like a mop, and drop you down a knot-hole, and nobody'd be the wiser."

The door now opened slowly and a small girl, miserably clad, entered the saloon. Her head was covered with a worn, soiled shawl. From underneath the shawl she produced a battered tin pail and placed it on the bar with the phlegmatic remark, "Pa wants a quart of beer."

Mrs. Burke looked at the girl and then at Bingham, and then back at the girl inquiringly.

"Are you in the habit of gettin' beer here, child?"

"Sure thing!" the girl replied, cheerfully.

"How old are you?"

"Ten, goin' on eleven."

"And you sell it to her?" Hepsey asked, turning to Bingham.

"Oh, it's for her father. He sends for it." He frowned at the child and she quickly disappeared, leaving the can behind her.

"Does he? But I thought you said that a saloon was no place for a woman; and surely it can't be a decent place for a girl under age. Now my friend, I've got somethin' to say to you."

"You are the very devil and all," Silas remarked.

"Thanks, Silas. The devil sticks to his job, anyway; and owin' to the likes of you he wins out, nine times out of ten. Now will you clear out of this location, or won't you?"

"Another day like this would send me to the lunatic asylum."

"Then I'll be around in the mornin' at six-thirty sharp."

"You just get out of here," he threatened.

"If you promise to clear out yourself within three days."

"I guess I'd clear out of Heaven itself to get rid of you."

"Very well; and if you are still here Saturday afternoon, ten of us women will come and sit on your steps until you go. A woman can't vote whether you shall be allowed to entice her men-folk into a place like this, and at the very church door; but the average woman can be mighty disagreeable when she tries."

Silas Bingham had a good business head: he reckoned up the costs — and cleared out.

CHAPTER XVII
NOTICE TO QUIT

Before the year was over Mrs. Betty had become popular with Maxwell's parishioners through her unfailing good-nature, cordiality and persistent optimism. Even Mrs. Nolan, who lived down by the bridge, and made rag carpets, and suffered from chronic dyspepsia, remarked to Mrs. Burke that she thought the parson's wife was very nice "'cause she 'aint a bit better than any of the rest of us,"—which tribute to Mrs. Betty's tact made Mrs. Burke smile and look pleased. All the young men and girls of the parish simply adored her, and it was marvelous how she managed to keep in touch with all the guilds, do her own housework, and learn to know everyone intimately. Hepsey warned her that she was attempting to do too much.

"The best parson's wife," she said, "is the one who makes the rest work, while she attends to her own household, and keeps her health. Her business is not to do the work of the parson, but to look after him, keep him well nourished, and cheer him up a little bit when he is tempted to take the next trolley for Timbuctoo."

The retort was so tempting that Mrs. Betty could not help saying:

"There's not a person in this town who does so much for others as you do, and who makes so little fuss about it. It's the force of your example that has led me astray, you see."

"Hm!" Hepsey replied. "I'm glad you called my attention to it. I shall try to break myself of the habit at once."

As for Maxwell, his practical helpfulness in forwarding the social life of the place, without in the least applying that phase of his activities as a lever for spiritual upheavals, and his ready sympathy for and interest in the needs and doings of young and old, irrespective of class or caste, gradualy reaped for him the affection and respect of all sorts and conditions. In fact, the year had been a pleasant one for him, and was marred by only one circumstance, the continued and growing hostility of his Senior Warden, Mr. Bascom. From the first, he had been distinctly unfriendly towards his rector; but soon after Maxwell's marriage, his annoying opposition was quite open and pronounced, and the weight of his personal influence was thrown against every move which Maxwell made towards the development of the parish life and work.

To those more "in the know" than the Maxwells themselves, it was evident that a certain keen aggressiveness evinced by the Senior Warden was foreign to his phlegmatic, brooding character, and it was clear to them that the actively malicious virus was being administered by the disappointed Virginia. That she was plotting punishment, in revenge for wounded *amour propre*, was clear to the initiated, who were apprehensive of the bomb she was evidently preparing to burst over the unconscious heads of the rector and his wife. But what could her scheme be?

Gradually Mrs. Burke noticed that Betty began to show fatigue and anxiety, and was losing the freshness of her delicate color; while Donald had become silent and reserved, and wore a worried look which was quite unnatural to him. Something was going wrong; of that she felt sure; but observant though she was, she failed to trace the trouble to its source.

Matters came to a crisis one day when Maxwell was informed that some one was waiting to see him in the parlor. The visitor was dressed in very pronounced clothes, and carried himself with a self-assertive swagger. Maxwell had seen him in Bascom's office, and knew who was waiting for him long before he reached the parlor, by the odor of patchouli which penetrated to the hall.

"Good morning, Mr. Nelson," said Maxwell. "Did you wish to see me?"

"Yes, I did, Mr. Maxwell, and I am sure it is a great pleasure."

The man seated himself comfortably in a large chair, put the tips of his fingers together, and gazed about the room with an expression of pleased patronage.

"Very pretty home you have here," he remarked suavely.

"Yes," Maxwell replied. "We manage to make ourselves comfortable. Did you wish to see me on business?"

"Oh yes," the lawyer replied, "a mere technicality. I represent the firm of Bascom & Nelson, or rather I should say I am Mr. Bascom's legal agent just at present, as I have not yet been admitted as his partner—"

The man stopped, smirked, and evidently relished prolonging his interview with Maxwell, who was getting impatient. Maxwell drew his watch from his pocket, and there was a look in his eyes which made the lawyer proceed:

"The fact is, Rector, that I came to see you on a matter of business about the rectory—as Mr. Bascom's agent."

"Will you kindly state it?"

"It concerns the use of this house."

"In what way? This is the rectory of the church, and the rental of it is part of my salary."

"You are mistaken. Mr. Bascom owns the house, and you are staying here merely on sufferance."

For a moment Maxwell was too astonished to speak; then he began:

"Mr. Bascom owns this house? What do you mean? The house is part of the property of the church."

"You are mistaken, my friend."

"You will kindly not repeat that form of address, and explain what you mean," replied Maxwell heatedly.

"Come, come; there's no use in losing your temper, my dear rector," retorted Nelson offensively.

"You have just two minutes to explain yourself, sir; and I strongly advise you to improve the opportunity, before I put you out of this house.'"

Nelson, like most bullies, was a coward, and evidently concluded that he would take no risks. He continued:

"As I said before, Sylvester Bascom practically owns this house. It does not belong to the church property. The Episcopals made a big bluff at buying it years ago, and made a very small payment in cash; Bascom took a mortgage for the rest. The interest was paid regularly for a while, and then payments began to fall off. As you have reason to know, Bascom is a generous and kind-hearted man, who would not for the world inconvenience his rector, and so he has allowed the matter to go by default, until the back interest amounts to a considerable sum. Of course the mortgage is long past due, and as he needs the money, he has commissioned me to see you and inform you that he is about to foreclose, and to ask you to vacate the premises as soon as you conveniently can. I hope that I make myself reasonably clear."

In a perfectly steady voice Maxwell replied:

"What you say is clear enough; whether it is true is another matter. I will see Mr. Bascom at once, and ask for his own statement of the case."

"I don't think it necessary to see him, as he has expressly authorized me to act for him in the case."

"Then I suppose you came her to serve the notice of ejectment on me."

"Oh, we won't use such strong language as that. I came here merely to tell you that the house must be vacated soon as possible. Mr.

Bascom has gone to New York on business and will not be back for two weeks. Meantime he wishes the house vacated, so that he can rent it to other parties."

"When does the Senior Warden propose to eject his rector, if I may be allowed to ask?"

"Oh, there is no immediate hurry. Any time this week will do."

"What does he want for this place?"

"I believe he expects fifteen dollars a month."

"Well, of course that is prohibitive. Tell Mr. Bascom that we will surrender the house on Wednesday, and that we are greatly indebted to him for allowing us to occupy it rent-free for so long a time."

As Donald showed the objectionable visitor out of the house, he caught sight of Hepsey Burke walking towards it. He half hoped she would pass by, but with a glance of suspicion and barely civil greeting to Nelson as he walked away, she came on, and with a friendly nod to Maxwell entered the rectory.

"I've just been talkin' to Mrs. Betty for her good," she remarked. "I met her in town, lookin' as peaked as if she'd been fastin' double shifts, and I had a notion to come in and complete the good work on yourself."

Maxwell's worried face told its own story. He was so nonplused by the bolt just dropped from the blue that he could find no words of responsive raillery wherewith to change the subject.

Hepsey led the way to the parlor and seated herself, facing him judicially. In her quick mind the new evidence soon crystallized into proof of her already half-formed suspicions. She came straight to the point.

"Is Bascom making you any trouble? If he is, say so, 'cause I happen to have the whip-hand so far as he's concerned. That Nelson's nothin' but a tool of his, and a dull tool at that."

"He's an objectionable person, I must say," remarked Maxwell, and hesitated to trust himself further.

Mrs. Burke gazed at Maxwell for some time in silence and then began:

"You look about done up—I don't want to be pryin', but I guess you'd better own up. Something's the matter."

"I am just worried and anxious, and I suppose I can't help showing it," he replied wearily.

"So you're worried, are you. Now don't you get the worried habit; if it makes a start it will grow on you till you find yourself worryin' for fear the moon won't rise. Worryin's like usin' rusty scissors: it sets your mouth awry. You just take things as they come, and when it seems as if everything was goin' to smash and you couldn't help it, put on your overalls and paint a fence, or hammer tacks, or any old thing that comes handy. What has that rascal Bascom been doin'? Excuse me—my diplomacy's of the hammer-and-tongs order; you're not gettin' your salary paid?"

For some time Maxwell hesitated and then answered:

"Well, I guess I might as well tell you, because you will know all about it anyway in a day or two, and you might as well get a correct version of the affair from me, though I hate awfully to trouble you. The parish owes me two hundred and fifty dollars. I spoke to Reynolds about it several times, but he says that Bascom and several of his intimate friends won't pay their subscriptions promptly, and so he can't pay me. But the shortage in my salary is not the worst of it. Did you know that the rectory was heavily mortgaged, and that Bascom holds the mortgage?"

"Yes, I knew it; but we paid something down', and the interest's been kept up, and we hoped that if we did that Bascom would be satisfied."

"It seems that the interest has not been paid in some time, and the real reason why Nelson called just now was to inform me that as

Bascom was about to foreclose we must get out as soon as we could. I told him that we would leave on Wednesday next."

For a moment there was a look on Mrs. Burke's face which Maxwell never had seen before, and which boded ill for Bascom: but she made no immediate reply.

"To tell you the truth," she said finally, "I have been afraid of this. That was the only thing that worried me about your gettin' married. But I felt that no good would come from worryin', and that if Bascom was goin' to play you some dirty trick, he'd do it; and now he's done it. What's got into the man, all of a sudden? He's a skinflint—always closer than hair to a dog's back; but I don't believe I've ever known him do somethin' downright ugly, like this."

"Oh, I know well enough," remarked Donald. "If I had been aware of how matters stood about the rectory, I should have acted differently. I wrote him a pretty stiff letter a day or two ago, calling upon him, as Senior Warden, to use his influence to fulfill the contract with me, and get the arrears of my salary paid up. I suppose he had thought I would just get out of the place if my salary was held back—and he's wanted to get rid of me for some time. Now, he's taken this other means of ejecting me not only from his house but from the town itself. He knows I can't afford to pay the rent out of my salary—let alone out of half of it!" He laughed rather bitterly.

"He'll be singing a different tune, before I've done with him," said Hepsey. "Now you leave this to me—I'll have a twitch on old Bascom's nose that'll make him think of something else than ejecting his rector. I'll go and visit with him a little this afternoon."

"But Nelson said that he was in New York."

"I know better than that," snorted Hepsey. "But I guess he'll want to go there, and stay the winter there too, maybe, when I've had my say. No sir—I'm goin' to take my knittin' up to his office, and sit awhile; and if he doesn't have the time of his life it won't be my fault."

She turned to leave the room, with a belligerent swing of her shoulders.

"Mrs. Burke," said Maxwell gently, "you are kindness itself; but I don't want you to do this—at least not yet. I want to fight this thing through myself, and rather to shame Bascom into doing the right thing than force him to do it—even if the latter were possible. I must think things out a bit. I shall want your help—we always do, Betty and I."

"I don't know but you're right; but if your plan don't work, remember mine *will*. Well, Mrs. Betty'll be coming in soon, and I'll leave you. Meantime I shall just go home and load my guns: I'm out for Bascom's hide, sooner or later."

CHAPTER XVIII
THE NEW RECTORY

When Betty returned, and Donald told her the happenings of the morning, the clouds dispersed somewhat, and before long the dictum that "there is humor in all things"—even in ejection from house and home—seemed proven true. After lunch they sat in Donald's den, and were laughingly suggesting every kind of habitat, possible and impossible, from purchasing and fitting up the iceman's covered wagon and perambulating round the town, to taking a store and increasing their income by purveying Betty's tempting preserves and confections.

Their consultation was interrupted by the arrival of Nickey, armed with a Boy Scouts' "Manual."

"Gee! Mr. Maxwell: Uncle Jonathan Jackson's all right; I'll never do another thing to guy him. He's loaned us his tent for our Boy Scouts' corpse, and I've been studyin' out how to pitch it proper, so I can show the kids the ropes; but—"

"Donald!" cried Betty. "The very thing—let's camp out on the church lot."

"By Jinks!" exclaimed Maxwell, unclerically. "We'll have that tent up this very afternoon—if Nickey will lend it to us, second hand, and get his men together."

Nickey flushed with delight. "You betcher life I will," he shouted excitedly. "Is it for a revival stunt? You 'aint goin' to live there, are you?"

"That's just what we are going to do, if Jonathan and you'll lend us the tent for a few months. Mr. Bascom wants to let the rectory to some other tenants, and we've got to find somewhere else to lay our heads. Why, it's the very way! There's not a thing against it, that I can see. Let's go and see the tent, and consult Mrs. Burke. Come along, both of you."

And off they hurried, like three children bent on a new game. It was soon arranged, and Hepsey rose to the occasion with her usual vim. To her and Nickey the transportation of the tent was consigned, while Maxwell went off to purchase the necessary boarding for a floor, and Mrs. Betty returned to the rectory to pack up their belongings.

"We'll have to occupy our new quarters to-night," said Maxwell, "or our friend the enemy may raid the church lot in the night, and vanish with tent and all."

An hour or so later, when Maxwell arrived at the church, clad in overalls and riding on a wagon of planks, he found Mrs. Burke and Nickey with a contingent of stalwarts awaiting him. There was a heap of canvas and some coils of rope lying on the ground near by. Hepsey greeted him with a smile from under the shade of her sunbonnet.

"You seem ready for business, even if you don't look a little bit like the Archbishop of Canterbury in that rig," she remarked. "I'm afraid there'll be an awful scandal in the parish if you go wanderin' around dressed like a carpenter; but it can't be helped; and if the Bishop excommunicates you, I'll give you a job on the farm."

"I don't mind about the looks of it; but I suppose the vestry will have something to say about our camping on church property."

"That needn't worry you. Maybe it'll bring 'em to their senses, and maybe, they'll be ashamed when they see their parson driven out of his house and havin' to live in a tent,—though I 'aint holdin' out much hope of that, to you. Folks that are the most religious are usually the hardest to shame. I always said, financially speakin', that preachin' wasn't a sound business. It's all give and no get; but this is the first time I've ever heard of a parish wanting a parson to preach without eating and to sleep without a roof over his head. Most of us seem to forget that rectors are human being like the rest of us. If religion is worth havin', it's worth payin' for."

The planking was soon laid, and the erection of the tent was left to Nickey's captaining—all hands assisting. With his manual in one hand he laid it out, rope by rope, poles in position, and each helper at his place. Then at a word, up it soared, with a "bravo" from the puzzled onlookers.

"We want a poet here," laughed Maxwell. "Longfellow's 'Building of the Ship,' or Ralph Connor's 'Building the Barn' aren't a circumstance to Nickey's 'Pitching the Parson's Tent.'"

It was next divided off into three convenient rooms, for sleeping, eating and cooking—and Hepsey, with three scouts, having driven across to the old rectory while the finishing touches were being put to the new, she and her military escort soon returned with Mrs. Betty, and a load of furniture and other belongings.

"Why, this is perfect!" cried Betty. "The only thing lacking to complete the illusion is a trout brook in the front yard, and the smell of pines and the damp mossy earth of the forests. We'll wear our old clothes, and have a bonfire at night, and roast potatoes and corn in the hot coals, and have the most beautiful time imaginable."

The town visitors who still lingered on the scene were received cordially by Maxwell and Mrs. Betty, who seemed to be in rather high spirits; but when the visitors made any inquiries concerning structural matters they were politely referred to Nickey Burke for any information they desired, as he had assumed official management of the work.

Just before the various helpers left at six o'clock, smoke began to issue from the little stove-pipe sticking out through the canvas of the rear of the tent, and Mrs. Betty, with her sleeves rolled up to her elbows and her cooking apron on, came out to watch it with all the pride of a good housekeeper.

"Isn't it jolly, Mrs. Burke," she exclaimed. "I was afraid that it would not draw, but it really does, you see. This will be more fun than a month at the seashore; and to-morrow we are going to have you and Nickey dine with us in the tent; so don't make any other engagement. Don't forget."

By noon of the following day everybody in town knew that the Maxwells had been dispossessed, and were camping on the church lot; and before night most of the women and a few of the men had called to satisfy their curiosity, and to express their sympathy with the rector and his wife, who, however, seemed to be quite comfortable and happy in their new quarters. On the other hand, some of the vestry hinted strongly that tents could not be put up on church property without their formal permission, and a few of the more pious suggested that it was little short of sacrilege thus to violate the sanctity of a consecrated place. Nickey had painted a large sign with the word RECTORY on it, in truly rustic lettering, and had hung it at the entrance of the tent. The Editor of the Durford Daily *Bugle* appeared with the village photographer, and after an interview with Maxwell requested him and his wife to pose for a picture in front of the tent. This they declined with thanks; but a half-column article giving a sensational account of the affair appeared in the next issue of the paper, headed by a half-tone picture of the tent and the church. Public sentiment ran strongly against Bascom, to whom rumor quickly awarded the onus of the incident. In reply to offers of hospitality, Maxwell and Mrs. Betty insisted that they were very comfortable for the time being, and were not going to move or make any plans for the immediate future. The morning of the fourth day, Maxwell announced to Mrs. Betty that he had a strong presentiment that Bascom would soon make another move in the game, and he was not surprised when he saw Nelson approaching.

"Thank goodness we are in the open air, this time," Maxwell remarked to Betty as he caught sight of the visitor. "I'll talk to him outside—and perhaps you'd better shut the door and keep out the language. I may have to express myself more forcibly than politely."

Nelson began:

"I am sorry to have to intrude upon you again, Mr. Maxwell, but I must inform you that you will have to vacant that tent and find lodgings elsewhere."

"Why, pray? This tent is my property for as long as I require it."

"Ah! But you see it has been put up on the land that belongs to the church, and you have no title to use the land, you know, for private purposes."

"Pardon me," Maxwell replied, "but while the legal title to all church property is held by the wardens and vestry collectively, the freehold use of the church building and grounds is held by the rector for the purpose of the exercise of his office as rector. No church property is injured by this tent. This lot was originally purchased for a rectory. To all intents and purposes (excuse me; I am not punning) this tent is the rectory *pro tem.* The use of a rectory was offered me as part of the original agreement when I accepted the call to come to this parish."

"Hm! You speak quite as if you belonged to the legal profession yourself, Mr. Maxwell. However, I am afraid that you will have to get off the lot just the same. You must remember that I am simply carrying out Mr. Bascom's instructions."

"Very well; please give my compliments to Mr. Bascom and tell him that he is welcome to come here and put me out as soon as he thinks best. Moreover, you might remind him that he is not an autocrat, and that he cannot take any legal action in the matter without a formal meeting of the vestry, which I will call and at which I will preside. He can appeal to the Bishop if he sees fit."

"Then I understand that you propose to stay where you are, in defiance of Mr. Bascom's orders?"

"I most certainly do. It is well known that Mr. Bascom has successfully intimidated every one of my predecessors; but he has met his match for once. I shall not budge from this tent until I see fit."

"Well, I should be very sorry to see you forcibly ejected."

"Don't waste any sympathy on me, sir. If Mr. Bascom attempts to molest me, I shall take the matter to the courts and sue him for damages."

"Your language is somewhat forcible, considering that you are supposed to be his pastor and spiritual advisor."

"Very well; tell Mr. Bascom that as his spiritual advisor I strongly suggest that his spiritual condition will not be much improved by attempting to molest us here."

"But to be perfectly frank with you, Mr. Maxwell, he can force you to leave, by stopping the payment of your salary, even if he does not eject you by force."

"I rather think not. Until he can bring specific charges against me, he is liable for the fulfillment of our original contract, in his writing. Moreover, I may have more friends in the parish than he imagines."

Nelson was visibly disturbed by the rector's firm hold on the situation.

"But," he stuttered, "Mr. Bascom is the richest man in the parish, and his influence is strong. You will find that everyone defers to his judgment as a matter of course."

"All right; then let me add, for your own information, that I can earn my living honestly in this town and take care of myself without Mr. Bascom's assistance, if necessary; and do my parish work at the same time. I have two muscular arms, and if it comes down to earning a livelihood, independent of my salary, I can work on the state road hauling stone. Williamson told me yesterday he was looking for men."

"I can scarcely think that the parishioners would hold with their rector working like a common laborer, Mr. Maxwell," admonished Nelson.

"We are all 'common,' in the right sense, Mr. Nelson. My view is that work of any kind is always honorable when necessary, except in the eyes of the ignorant. If Mr. Bascom is mortified to have me earn my living by manual labor, when he is not ashamed to repudiate a contract, and try to force me out of the parish by a process of slow starvation, his sense of fitness equals his standard of honor."

"Well, I am sure that I do not know what I can do."

"Do you want me to tell you?"

"If it will relieve your feelings," Nelson drawled insolently.

"Then get out of this place and stay out. If you return again for any purpose whatever I am afraid it is I who will have to eject you. We will not argue the matter again."

"Well, I regret this unfortunate encounter, and to have been forced to listen to the unguarded vituperation of my rector." With which retort he departed.

Soon after Nelson had left, Mrs. Burke called in, and Betty gave her a highly amusing and somewhat colored version of the interview.

"You know, I think that our theological seminaries don't teach budding parsons all they ought to, by any means," she concluded.

"I quite agree with you, Betty dear; and I thank my stars for college athletics," laughed Maxwell, squaring up to the tent-pole.

"What did I tell you," reminded Hepsey, "when you had all those books up in your room at my place. It's just as important for a country parson to know how to make a wiped-joint or run a chicken farm or pull teeth, as it is to study church history and theology. A parson's got to live somehow, and a trade school ought to be attached to every seminary, according to my way of thinking! St. Paul made tents, and wasn't a bit ashamed of it. Well I'm mighty glad that Bascom has got come up with for once. Don't you give in, and it will be my turn to make the next move, if this don't bring him to his senses. You just wait and see."

CHAPTER XIX

COULEUR de ROSE

Hepsey had been so busy with helping the Maxwells that for some time no opportunity had occurred for Jonathan to press his ardent suit. Since his first attempt and its abrupt termination, he had been somewhat bewildered; he had failed to decide whether he was an engaged man open to congratulations, or a rejected suitor to be condoled with. He tried to recall exactly what she had said. As near as he could recollect, it was: "I'll think it over, and perhaps some day—" Then he had committed the indiscretion of grasping her hand, causing her to drop her stitches before she had ended what she was going to say. He could have sworn at himself to think that it was all his fault that she had stopped just at the critical moment, when she might have committed herself and given him some real encouragement. But he consoled himself by the thought that she had evidently taken him seriously at last; and so to the "perhaps some day" he added, in imagination, the words "I will take you"; and this seemed reasonable.

The matter was more difficult from the very fact that they had been on such intimate terms for such a long time, and she had never hitherto given him any reason to think that she cared for him other than as a good neighbor and a friend. Ever since the death of his wife, she seemed to feel that he had been left an orphan in a cold and unsympathetic world, and that it was her duty to look after him much as she would a child. She was in the habit of walking over whenever she pleased and giving directions to Mary McGuire in regard to matters which she thought needed attention in his house. And all this had been done in the most open and matter-of-fact way, so that the most accomplished gossip in Durford never accused her of making matrimonial advances to the lonesome widower. Even Jonathan himself had been clever enough to see that she regarded him much as she would an overgrown boy, and had always accepted her many attentions without misinterpreting them. She was a born manager, and she managed him; that was all. Nothing could be more unsentimental than the way in which she would make him take off his coat during a friendly call, and let her sponge and press it for him; or the imperative fashion in which she sent him to the barber's to have his beard trimmed. How could a man make love to a woman after she had acted like this?

But he reminded himself that if he was ever to win her he must begin to carry out the advice outlined by Mrs. Betty; and so the apparently unsuspecting Hepsey would find on her side porch in the morning some specially fine corn which had been placed there after dark without the name of the donor. Once a fine melon was accompanied by a bottle of perfumery; and again a basket of peaches had secreted in its center a package of toilet soap "strong enough to kill the grass," as Hepsey remarked as she sniffed at it. Finally matters reached a climax when a bushel of potatoes arrived on the scene in the early dawn, and with it a canary bird in a tin cage. When Hepsey saw Jonathan later, she remarked casually that she "guessed she'd keep the potatoes; but she didn't need a canary bird any more than a turtle needs a tooth-pick; and he had better take it away and get his money back."

However, Jonathan never allowed her occasional rebuffs to discourage him or stop his attentions. He kept a close watch on all Hepsey's domestic interests, and if there were any small repairs to be made at Thunder Cliff, a hole in the roof to be mended, or the bricks on the top of the chimney to be relaid, or the conductor pipe to be readjusted, Jonathan was on the spot. Then Jonathan would receive in return a layer cake with chopped walnuts in the filling, and would accept it in the same matter-of-fact way in which Hepsey permitted his services as general caretaker.

This give-and-take business went on for some time. At last it occurred to him that Mrs. Burke's front porch ought to be painted, and he conceived the notion of doing the work without her knowledge, as a pleasant surprise to her. He waited a long time for some day when she should be going over to shop at Martin's Junction,—when Nickey usually managed to be taken along,—so that he could do the work unobserved. Meantime, he collected from the hardware store various cards with samples of different colors on them. These he would combine and re-combine at his leisure, in the effort to decide just what colors would harmonize. He finally decided that a rather dark blue for the body work would go quite well, with a bright magenta for the trimmings, and laid in a stock of paint and brushes, and possessed his soul in patience.

So one afternoon, arriving home burdened with the spoils of Martin's Junction, great was Mrs. Burke's astonishment and wrath when she discovered the porch resplendent in dark blue and magenta.

"Sakes alive! Have I got to live inside of that," she snorted. "Why, it's the worst lookin' thing I ever saw. If I don't settle *him*," she added, "—paintin' my porch as if it belonged to him—and me as well," she added ambiguously. And, catching up her sun-bonnet, she hastened over to her neighbor's and inquired for Jonathan. "Sure, he's gone to Martin's Junction to see his brother, Mrs. Burke. He said he'd stay over night, and I needn't come in again till to-morrow dinner-time," Mary McGuire replied.

Hepsey hastened home, and gathering all the rags she could find, she summoned Nickey and Mullen, one of the men from the farm, and they worked with turpentine for nearly two hours, cleaning off the fresh paint from the porch. Then she sent Nickey down to the hardware store for some light gray paint and some vivid scarlet paint, and a bit of dryer. It did not take very long to repaint her porch gray—every trace of the blue and the magenta having been removed by the vigorous efforts of the three.

When it was finished, she opened the can of scarlet, and pouring in a large quantity of dryer she sent Nickey over to see if Mary McGuire had gone home. All three set to work that evening to paint the porch in front of Jonathan's house. At first Mullen protested anxiously that it was none of his business to be painting another man's porch, but Mrs. Burke gave him a look which changed his convictions; so he and Nickey proceeded gleefully to fulfill their appointed task, while she got supper.

When the work was quite finished. Hepsey went over to inspect it, and remarked thoughtfully to herself: "I should think that a half pint of dryer might be able to get in considerable work before to-morrow noon. I hope Jonathan'll like scarlet. To be sure it does look rather strikin' on a white house; but then variety helps to relieve the monotony of a dead alive town like Durford; and if he don't like it plain, he can trim it green. I'll teach him to come paintin' my house without so much as a by-your-leave, or with-your-leave, lettin' the whole place think things."

As it happened, Jonathan returned late that night to Durford—quite too late to see the transformation of his own front porch, and since he entered by the side door as usual, he did not even smell the new paint. The next morning he sauntered over to Thunder Cliff, all agog for his reward, and Mrs. Burke greeted him at her side door, smiling sweetly.

"Good mornin', Jonathan. It was awful good of you to paint my front porch. It *has* needed paintin' for some time now, but I never seemed to get around to it."

"Don't mention it, Hepsey," Jonathan replied affably. "Don't mention it. You're always doin' somethin' for me, and it's a pity if I can't do a little thing like that for you once in a while."

Hepsey had strolled round to the front, as if to admire his work, Jonathan following. Suddenly he came to a halt; his jaw dropped, and he stared as if he had gone out of his senses.

"Such a lovely color; gray just suits the house, you know," Mrs. Burke observed. "You certainly ought to have been an artist,

Jonathan. Any man with such an eye for color ought not to be wastin' his time on a farm."

Jonathan still gazed at the porch in amazement, blinked hard, wiped his eyes and his glasses with his handkerchief, and looked again.

"What's the matter with you? Have you a headache?" Hepsey inquired solicitously.

"No, I haven't got no headache; but when I left that porch yesterday noon it was blue, and now I'm blamed if it don't seem gray. Does it look gray-like to you, Hepsey?"

"Why certainly! What's that you say? Do you say you painted it blue? That certainly's mighty queer. But then you know some kinds of paint fade—some kinds do!" She nodded, looking suspiciously at the work.

"Fade!" Jonathan sneered. "Paints don't fade by moonlight in one night. That isn't no faded blue. It's just plain gray. I must be goin' color blind, or something."

"It looks gray to me, and I'm glad it is gray, so don't you worry about it, Jonathan. Blue would be somethin' awful on the front of a white house, you know."

"Well," continued the bewildered Junior Warden, "I'm blessed if this isn't the queerest thing I ever see in all my born days. If I catch the fellow that sold me that paint, I'll make it lively for him or my name isn't Jackson."

"Oh, I wouldn't do anything like that! What difference does it make, so long as I like the color myself; it's my house. I should have been very much put out if you'd painted it blue; yes, I should."

"But I don't like to be cheated down at the store; and I won't, by gum! They said it was best quality paint! I'll go down to Crosscut's and see about this business, right now. I've traded with him nigh on twenty years, and he don't bamboozle me that way."

Hepsey turned away choking with laughter, and retreated to her kitchen.

Jonathan started back towards his house to get his hat and coat, and then for the first time he caught sight of his own porch, done in flaming scarlet, which fairly seemed to radiate heat in the brilliant sunlight. He stood motionless for nearly a minute, paralyzed. Then the color began to rise in his neck and face as he muttered under his breath:

"Hm! I'm on to the whole business now. I ought to have known that Hepsey would get the best of me. I guess I won't go down to Crosscut's after all."

Then he walked up to the porch and touched the scarlet paint with his finger and remarked:

"Set harder than a rock, by gum! She must have used a whole lot of dryer. I'll get even with her for this. See if I don't."

In the afternoon Jonathan brought over some fine apples and presented them to Hepsey, who was knitting on her side porch. She thanked him for the gift, and the conversation drifted from one thing to another while she waited for the expected outburst of reproach which she knew would come sooner or later. But curiously enough, Jonathan was more cheery and cordial than usual, and made no allusion whatever to the scarlet porch, which was conspicuously visible from where they sat. Again and again Hepsey led the conversation around to the point where it seemed as if he must break covert, but he remained oblivious, and changed the subject readily. Not a word on the subject passed his lips that afternoon.

Then, from day to day the neighbors called and inquired of her if Jackson had gone off his head, or what was the matter. His flaming porch outraged Durford's sense of decency. She was at her wits end to answer, without actually lying or compromising herself; so the only thing she said was that she had noticed that he had been acting a bit peculiar lately, now they mentioned it. As time went on, the scarlet porch became the talk of the town. It was duly discussed at the sewing society, and the reading club, and the general sentiment was practically unanimous that Jackson must be suffering from incipient cataract or senile dementia, and needed a guardian. Even Mary McGuire remarked to Mrs. Burke that she was afraid "that there front porch would sure set the house on fire, if it wasn't put out before." Everybody agreed that if his wife had lived, the thing never could have happened.

Meantime, Jonathan went about his daily business, serene and happy, apparently oblivious of the fact that there was anything unusual in the decoration of his house. When his friends began to chaff him about the porch he seemed surprised, and guessed it was his privilege to paint his house any color he had a mind to, and there was no law ag'in' it; it was nobody's business but his own. Tastes in color differed, and there was no reason in the world why all houses should be painted alike. He liked variety himself, and nobody could say that scarlet wasn't a real cheerful color on a white house.

Occasionally people who were driving by stopped to contemplate the porch; and the Durford Daily *Bugle* devoted a long facetious paragraph to the matter. All of which Mrs. Burke knew very well, and it was having its effect on her nerves. The porch was the most conspicuous object in view from Hepsey's sitting-room windows, and every time she entered the room she found herself looking at the flaming terror with increasing exasperation. Verily, if Jonathan wanted revenge he was getting far more than he knew: the biter was badly bit. The matter came to a crisis one day, when Jonathan concluded a discussion with Mrs. Burke about the pasture fence. She burst out abruptly:

"Say, Jonathan Jackson, why in the name of conscience don't you paint your porch a Christian color? It's simply awful, and I'm not goin' to sit in my house and have to look at it all winter."

Jonathan did not seem greatly stirred, and replied in an absent-minded way:

"Why don't you move your sittin' room over to the other side of the house, Hepsey? Then you wouldn't have to see it. Don't you like scarlet?"

"No, I don't like it, and if you don't paint it out, I will."

"Don't do nothin' rash, Hepsey. You know sometimes colors fade in the moonlight—some colors, that is. Maybe that scarlet porch'll turn to a light gray if you let it alone."

Mrs. Burke could stand it no longer; so, laying down her work she exploded her pent-up wrath:

"Jonathan Jackson, if that paint isn't gone before to-morrow, I'll come over and paint it myself."

"Oh, that isn't necessary, Hepsey. And it might set people talkin'. But if you won't move your sittin'-room to the other side of your own house, why don't you move it over to my house? You wouldn't see so much of the red paint then."

Hepsey snorted and spluttered in baffled rage.

"Now, now, Hepsey," soothed Jonathan, "if that don't suit you, I'll tell you what I'll do: I'll paint it over myself on one condition!"

"And what's that, I'd like to know?"

"That you'll marry me," snapped Jonathan hungrily.

Instead of resenting such bold tactics on the part of her suitor, Mrs. Burke gazed at him a long time with a rather discouraged look on her face.

"Land sakes!" she exclaimed at last with assumed weariness and a whimsical smile, "I didn't know I'd ever come to this; but I guess I'll have to marry you to keep you from makin' another kind of fool of yourself; widowers are such helpless mortals, and you certainly do need a guardian." She shook her head at him despondently.

Jonathan advanced towards her deliberately, and clinched the matter:

"Well, Hepsey, seein' that we're engaged—"

"Engaged? What do you mean? Get away, you—" She rose from her chair in a hurry.

"Now Hepsey, a bargain's a bargain: you just said you'd have to marry me, and I guess the sooner you do it and have it over with, the better. So, seein' that we are engaged to be married, as I was about to remark when you interrupted me...." Relentlessly he approached her once more. She retreated a step or two.

"Well! Sakes alive, Jonathan! Whatever's come over you to make you so masterful. Well, yes then—I suppose a bargain's a bargain, all right. But before your side of it's paid up you've got to go right over and paint that porch of yours a respectable color."

So, for once, Hepsey's strategy had been manipulated to her own defeat: Jonathan went off to town with flying colors, and bought himself a can of pure white paint.

CHAPTER XX

MUSCULAR CHRISTIANITY

It was eleven o'clock at night. Mrs. Betty had retired, while her husband was still struggling to finish a sermon on the importance of foreign missions. Ordinarily, the work would have been congenial and easy for him, because he was an enthusiast in the matter of missionary work: but now for some reason his thoughts were confused; his enthusiasm was lacking, and his pen dragged. He tried hard to pull himself together, but over and over again the question kept repeating itself in his tired brain: Why should the Church support foreign missions, while she lets her hard working clergy at home suffer and half starve in their old age, and even fails to give them decent support while they are working in their prime? Why should a doctor reach his highest professional value at seventy, and a parson be past the "dead-line" at forty-five? Here he was, subject to the caprice and ill-will of a sour and miserly Senior Warden, and a cowed and at least partially "bossed" vestry—and he, the rector, with no practical power of appeal for the enforcement of his legal contract. It was only thanks to Jonathan Jackson, the Junior Warden, that any revenue at all reached him; for Bascom had used every grain of influence he possessed to reduce or stop Maxwell's salary. Mrs. Betty, plucky and cheery though she was, already showed the results of the weary struggle: it was not the work that took the color from her cheeks and the freshness from her face, but the worry incidental to causes which, in any other calling in life but his, would be removable.

Already he had parted with a considerable number of his books to eke out, and meet the many calls upon him—urgent and insistent calls. It became abundantly clear, as his mind strayed from the manuscript before him and turned to their immediate situation, that he was already forced to choose between two alternatives: either he must give up, and own himself and all the better influences in the place beaten by Bascom and his satellites; or he must find some means of augmenting his means of living, without allowing his time and energy to be monopolized to the neglect of essential parish and church duties.

As he thought on these things, somehow his enthusiasm for foreign missions ebbed away, and left him desperately tired and worried. He made several abortive attempts to put some fire into his missionary plea, but it was useless; and he was about to give up when he heard Mrs. Betty's gentle voice inquiring from the next room:

"May I come in? Haven't you finished that wretched old missionary sermon yet?"

"No, dear; but why aren't you asleep?"

"I have been anxious about you. You are worn out and you need your rest. Now just let the heathen rage, and go to bed."

Maxwell made no reply, but picked at his manuscript aimlessly with his pen. Betty looked into his face, and then the whole stress of the situation pierced her; and sitting down by his side she dropped her head on his shoulder and with one arm around his neck stroked his cheek with her fingers. For a few moments neither of them spoke; and then Maxwell said quietly:

"Betty, love, I am going to work."

"But Donny, you are one of the hardest working men in this town. What do you mean?"

"Oh, I mean that I am going to find secular work, the work of a day laborer, if necessary. Matters have come to a crisis, and I simply cannot stand this sort of thing any longer. If I were alone I might get along; but I have you, sweetheart, and—"

Maxwell stopped suddenly, and the brave little woman at his side said:

"Yes, I know all about it, Donald, and I think you are fully justified in doing anything you think best."

"And you wouldn't feel ashamed of me if I handled a shovel or dug in the street?"

"I'd be the proudest woman in the town, Donny; you are just your fine dear self, whatever you do; and if you have the courage to put your pride in your pocket and work in overalls, that would make you all the finer to me. Manual work would relieve the tension of your nerves. You seem to be in fairly good physical condition. Don't you worry one bit about me. I am going to wash some lace curtains for Mrs. Roscoe-Jones, and that will keep me out of mischief. Now, if you will allow me, I am going to tear up that sermon on foreign missions, and start a little home mission of my own by sending you to bed."

The second morning after this ruthless destruction of Maxwell's eloquent plea for the mission at Bankolulu, Danny Dolan drove up to the tent-rectory at half-past six, and Maxwell emerged and jumped up by Danny's side, dressed in a rather soiled suit of overalls: Danny was a teamster, a good looking youth, and a devoted friend of Maxwell's since the parson had taken care of him and his family through an attack of malignant diphtheria. But while Danny was a most loyal friend, he was not of the emotional type, and so, when Maxwell had seated himself comfortably and had lighted his briar pipe, Danny started down the road at a vigorous pace, grinning broadly at Maxwell's attire as he remarked:

"So you're really goin' to work like the rest of us, I reckon."

"Right you are, Danny—four days a week, anyhow. Don't I look like the real thing?"

"Sure you do; only you better not shave every day, and you'll have to get your hands dirty before you can fool anybody, and maybe your face'll give you away even then. Be you comfortable in them clothes?"

"Sure thing; I'm never so contented as I am in working clothes."

"That's all right. You're the stuff. But how about the proper old maids in the parish who ogle and dance around you; they won't cotton to your clothes a little bit. They'll think you're degradin' of yourself and disgracin' of the parish. Here you be ridin' on a stone wagon, and you don't look a bit better than me, if I do say it."

"I'm afraid they'll have to survive the shock somehow or other; a man has to dress according to his work."

"Hm! Now there's that there Mrs. Roscoe-Jones and Miss Bascom; I'll bet if they saw you in that rig they'd throw a fit."

"Oh no; it isn't as bad as that, Danny."

"They'd think you'd been disgraced for life, to become a laborin' man, you bet."

"A what?"

"A laborin' man."

"Then you think that a parson doesn't labor?"

"Well, I always thought that bein' a parson was a dead easy job, and a nice clean job too."

"Danny," Maxwell inquired after a momentary silence, "don't you suppose that a man labors with his brain as well as with his muscles? And sometimes a parson labors with his heart, and that is the hardest kind of work a man ever does. The man who is most of a laboring man is the man who labors with every power and faculty he possesses."

"Well, now, I guess that may be right, if you look at it that way."

"Yes; you speak of a laboring man, and you mean a man who uses his muscles and lets his brain and his feelings die of starvation. To try to help some one you're fond of, who is going to the bad, is the most nerve-racking and exhausting work which any man can possibly do."

"Hm! you always was a dum queer parson, more like the rest of us, somehow. And you don't hold that you're disgracin' your profession ridin' with me, and shovelin' gravel?"

"I don't seem to be worrying much about it, do I?"

"No," he agreed—and added, "and I'm dum sure I would like a day off now and then from preachin' and callin' on old maids, if I was you. But there's times I might be willin' for to let you take my work for yours."

"Now see here, if you'll do my work for a few days, I'll do yours."

"Well, what'd I have to do? I 'aint makin' any contract without specifications."

"Well, suppose we say you do my work Saturday and Sunday. That means you finish up two sermons, which must be original and interesting when you are preaching to the same set of people about a hundred and fifty times a year. Then you must go and see a woman who is always complaining, and listen to her woes for three-quarters of an hour. Then you must go and see what you can do for Tom Bradsaw, who is dying of tuberculosis. Then you must conduct a choir rehearsal—not always the highest gratification of a musical ear. Sunday, you must conduct four services and try to rouse a handful of people, who stare at you from the back pews, to some higher ideals of life and common decency, Then—"

"Oh, heavens, man! Sure, an' that's enough; I stick to the stone wagon every time."

"You'd be a fool if you didn't," replied Maxwell straightly. "Then again you get your pay promptly every Saturday night. I never know when I am going to get mine."

"You don't? Begad, and I wouldn't work for anybody if I wasn't paid prompt. I'd sue the Bishop or the Pope, or somebody."

"Parsons don't sue: it's considered improper."

"Well, well," muttered the astonished Danny. "Be you sure you can shovel stone then?" he asked.

Maxwell unbuttoned his wristband, rolled up his sleeve. "If I can't, I'll know the reason why," he remarked tersely.

"That's the stuff," laughed Danny, looking at Maxwell's muscle. "I guess I don't want to meet you out walkin' after dark without a gun. But say, why don't you swat the Bishop one, and get your pay?"

"The Bishop isn't responsible."

"Well, I'll bet I know who is, dang him; and I'd like to swat him one for you, the miserable old bag-of-bones."

"Never you mind, Danny; I can take care of myself."

"Sure you can, and I guess you're a laborin' man all right, even if you don't belong to the Union. Why don't you get up a parson's Union and go on strike? By Jove! I would. Let your parish go to—"

"Danny, don't you think it looks like rain?"

"No, neither do you; but here we are at the stone pile. My! but how the fellers will grin when they see a tenderfoot like you, and a parson at that, shovelin' stone. But they won't think any the less of you for it, mind you," he reassured his companion.

Maxwell knew most of the men, and greeted them by name, and when he rolled up his sleeves and began work, they quickly saw that he was "no slouch," and that he did not "soldier," or shirk, as many of them did—though sometimes they were inclined to rest on their shovels and chaff him good-naturedly, and ask him if he had his Union card with him.

Shoveling stone is no picnic, as Danny and his fellows would have put it. It is not only the hard, obstructed thrust, thrust of the shovel into the heap of broken stone, and the constant lift and swing of each shovelful into the wagon; it is the slow monotony of repetition of unvarying motion that becomes most irksome to the tyro, and wears down the nervous system of the old hand till his whole being is leveled to the insensibility of a soulless machine.

But, though new to the process itself, Maxwell was not ignorant of its effects; and soon he found himself distracting his attention from the strain of the muscular tension by fitting the action to the rhythm of some old sailor's chanteys he had learned at college. The effect amused the men; and then as some of them caught the beat, and others joined in, soon the whole gang was ringing the changes on the simple airs, and found it a rousing and cheerful diversion from the monotony of labor.

If a pause came, soon one of them would call out: "Come on, Parson; strike up the hymn."

One by one the wagons were loaded, and driven to the road. After they had filled the last wagon, Danny put on his coat, and he and Maxwell mounted and drove out of the yard.

"Where are we going with this?" Maxwell inquired.

"Down on the state road, first turn to the left."

"Why, that must be near Willow Bluff, Mr. Bascom's place, isn't it?"

"Right opposite. Bascom, he come out yesterday, and said he wouldn't stand for that steam roller snortin' back and forth in front of his house. But Jim Ferris told him he had his orders from Williamson, and he wasn't goin' to be held up by nobody until Williamson told him to stop. Jim isn't any kind of fool."

When they arrived in front of Willow Bluff, they stopped, dismounted, and dumped the crushed stone, and then returned to the stone yard. At noon they camped out on the curb in front of Willow Bluff. After Maxwell had done full justice to the contents of his dinner pail, he stretched himself full length on the grass for a few moments, chatting with his mates in friendly fashion. Then he went over to the roller and assisted the engineer in "oiling up." Being a novice at the business, he managed to get his hands black with oil, and smeared a streak across one cheek, which, while it helped to obscure his identity, did not add to his facial beauty. He was blissfully unconscious of this. About three o'clock Bascom returned from his office, just as Maxwell was dismounting from the wagon after bringing a load. At first Bascom did not recognize the rector, but a second glance brought the awful truth home to his subliminal self, and he stopped and stared at Maxwell, stricken dumb. Maxwell politely touched his hat, and smilingly remarked that it was a fine day. Bascom made no reply at first.

"I CONSIDER IT A SHAME AND A DISGRACE TO THE PARISH TO HAVE OUR RECTOR IN FILTHY CLOTHES, DRAWING STONE WITH A LOT OF RUFFIANS"

"Can it be possible that this is you, Mr. Maxwell?" he almost whispered, at last.

"It is, to the best of my knowledge and belief."

"What in the name of heaven are you working with these men for, if I may ask?"

"To earn sufficient money to pay my grocer's bill."

Bascom colored hotly, and sputtered:

"I consider it a shame and a disgrace to the parish to have our rector in filthy clothes, drawing stone with a lot of ruffians."

Maxwell colored as hotly, and replied:

"They are not ruffians, sir; they are honest men, supporting their families in a perfectly legitimate way, giving their labor and"— significantly—"receiving their pay for it."

"And you, sir, are engaged to work for the parish, as a minister of God."

"Unfortunately, I am not being paid by the parish; that is why I am working here. Neither my wife nor myself is going to starve."

"You haven't any pride, sir!" Bascom fumed, his temper out of control. "We have had many incompetent rectors, but this really surpasses anything. We have never had anyone like you."

Maxwell paused again in his work, and, leaning on his shovel, looked Bascom in the eye:

"By which you mean that you have never had anyone who was independent enough to grip the situation in both hands and do exactly what he thought best, independent of your dictation."

"I will not converse with you any more. You are insulting."

"As the corporation is paying me for my time, I prefer work to conversation."

Bascom strode along the road towards his home. Danny Dolan, who had been a shameless auditor of this conversation, from the other side of the wagon, was beside himself with delight:

"Holy Moses! but didn't you give it to the old man. And here be all your adorers from town after comin' to tea at the house, and you lookin' like the stoker of an engine with black grease half an inch thick on your cheek."

Maxwell pulled out his handkerchief, and made an abortive effort to get his face clean.

"How is it now, Danny?"

"Oh, it 'aint nearly as thick in any one place; it's mostly all over your face now." Then Danny laughed irreverently again. "Sure, an' you certainly do look like the real thing now."

Maxwell was raking gravel when the guests for the afternoon tea were passing; and though he did not look up, he fully realized that they had recognized him, from the buzz of talk and the turning of heads.

Danny returned from his safer distance when he saw the coast was clear. Maxwell had a shrewd suspicion that the boy had taken himself off believing it might embarrass Maxwell less if any of the ladies should speak to him.

"Did none of 'em know you, then?" he asked.

"Not one of them spoke; I guess my disguise is pretty complete."

"Thank hiven!" Danny exclaimed. "Then the crisis is passed for to-day at least, and your reputation is saved; but if you don't get out of this they'll be comin' out again, and then nobody knows what'll happen. Better smear some more oil over the other cheek to cover the last bit of dacency left in you."

At the end of the day's work, Maxwell threw his shovel into Dolan's wagon and jumped up on the seat with him and drove back to town.

"Well," said Maxwell's friend, delightedly, "you done a mighty good day's work for a tenderfoot; but you done more with that old Bascom than in all the rest of the day put together. My! but I thought I'd split my sides to see you puttin' him where he belonged, and you lookin' like a coal heaver. But it's a howlin' shame you didn't speak to them women, goin' all rigged up for the party. That would've been the finishin' touch."

He swayed about on his seat, laughing heartily, until they drew up before the rectory, where Mrs. Betty was waiting to greet Maxwell.

Danny touched his cap shyly—but Betty came down to the wagon and gave him a cheery greeting.

"Well—you've brought him back alive, Mr. Dolan, anyway."

"Yes ma'am! And I reckon he'll keep you busy puttin' the food to him, if he eats like he works: he's a glutton for work, is Mr. Maxwell."

CHAPTER XXI
UNINVITED GUESTS

A few nights later, when Maxwell returned from his work he found Mrs. Burke sitting on the front platform of the tent with Mrs. Betty; and having washed, and changed his clothes, he persuaded their visitor to stay to supper. After supper was over they sat out doors, chatting of Maxwell's amusing experiences.

They had not been sitting long when their attention was attracted by a noise up the street, and going to the fence they saw a horse, over which the driver evidently had lost control, galloping towards them, with a buggy which was swerving from side to side under the momentum of its terrific speed.

Maxwell rushed into the middle of the street to see if he could be of any assistance in stopping the horse and preventing a catastrophe; but before he could get near enough to be of any service the animal suddenly shied, the buggy gave a final lurch, overturned, and was thrown violently against a telegraph pole. The horse, freed, dashed on, dragging the shafts and part of the harness. The occupant of the buggy had been thrown out against the telegraph pole with considerable force, knocked senseless, and lay in the gutter, stained with blood and dirt. Mrs. Burke and Betty lifted the body of the buggy, while Maxwell pulled out from under it the senseless form of a man; and when they had turned him over and wiped the blood from his face, they discovered, to their utter amazement, that the victim was no less a personage than the Senior Warden, Sylvester Bascom.

Of course there was nothing to be done but to carry him as best they could into the tent, and lay him on a lounge. Maxwell ran hastily for a doctor, while Hepsey and Mrs. Betty applied restoratives, washed the face of the injured man, and bound up as best they could what appeared to be a serious wound on one wrist, and another on the side of his head. The doctor responded promptly, and after a thorough examination announced that Bascom was seriously hurt, and that at present it would be dangerous to remove him. So Mrs. Betty and her guest removed Maxwell's personal belongings, and improvised a bed in the front room of the tent, into which Bascom was lifted with the greatest care. Having done what he could, the doctor departed, promising to return soon. In about twenty minutes there were signs of returning consciousness, and for some time Bascom looked about him in a dazed way, and groaned with pain. Mrs. Burke decided at once to remain all night with Mrs. Betty, and assist in caring for the warden until Virginia could arrive and assume charge of the case. After about an hour, Bascom seemed to be fully conscious as he gazed from one face to another, and looked wonderingly at the canvas tent in which he found himself. Mrs. Burke bent over him and inquired:

"Are you in much pain, Mr. Bascom?"

For a moment or two the Senior Warden made no answer; then in a hoarse whisper he inquired:

"Where am I? What has happened?"

"Well, you see, something frightened your horse, and your buggy was overturned, and you were thrown against a telegraph pole and injured more or less. We picked you up and brought you in here, cleaned you up, and tried to make you as comfortable as possible. The doctor has been here and looked you over, and will return in a few minutes."

"Am I seriously injured?"

"You have two bad wounds, and have evidently lost a good deal of blood; but don't worry. Mrs. Betty and I and the rest of us will take good care of you and do all we can until Virginia is able to take you home again."

"Where am I?"

A curious expression of mild triumph and amusement played across Mrs. Burke's face as she replied:

"You are in Donald Maxwell's tent. This was the nearest place where we could bring you at the time of the accident."

For a moment a vestige of color appeared in Bascom's face, and he whispered hoarsely:

"Why didn't you take me home?"

"Well, we were afraid to move you until the doctor had examined you thoroughly."

The patient closed his eyes wearily.

It was evident that he was growing weaker, and just as the doctor returned, he again lapsed into unconsciousness. The doctor felt of Bascom's pulse, and sent Maxwell hastily for Doctor Field for consultation. For fifteen minutes the doctors were alone in Bascom's room, and then Doctor Field called Maxwell in and quietly informed him that the warden had lost so much blood from the wound in the wrist that there was danger of immediate collapse unless they resorted to extreme measures, and bled some one to supply the patient. To this Maxwell instantly replied:

"I am strong and well. There is no reason why you should hesitate for a moment. Send for your instruments at once; but my wife must know nothing of it until it is all over with. Tell Mrs. Burke to take her over to Thunder Cliff for an hour or two, on the pretext of getting some bedding. Yes, I insist on having my own way, and as you say, there is no time to be lost."

Doctor Field took Mrs. Burke aside, and the women immediately departed for Thunder Cliff. The necessary instruments were brought, and then the three men entered the sick room.

In about twenty minutes Maxwell came out of the invalid's room, assisted by Doctor Field, and stretched himself on the bed.

Bascom's color began slowly to return; his pulse quickened, and Dr. Field remarked to his colleague:

"Well, I think the old chap is going to pull through after all; but it was a mighty close squeak."

Meanwhile, the messenger who had been sent out to Willow Bluff to apprise Virginia of her father's accident returned with the information that Virginia had left the day before, to stay with friends, and could not possibly get home till next day. It was decided to telegraph for her; and in the meantime the doctors advised that Mr. Bascom be left quietly in his bed at the new "rectory," and be moved home next day, after having recovered some of his lost strength. Mrs. Betty and Mrs. Burke took turns in watching by the invalid that night, and it might have been observed that his eyes remained closed, even when he did not sleep, while Mrs. Burke was in attendance, but that he watched Mrs. Betty with keen curiosity and wonder, from between half-closed lids, as she sat at the foot of his bed sewing, or moved about noiselessly preparing the nourishment prescribed for him by the doctors, and which the old gentleman took from her with unusual gentleness and patience.

It was Mrs. Burke who, having learned of the time when Virginia was expected to return home, drove out to Willow Bluff with Mr. Bascom, and assisted in making him comfortable there before his daughter's arrival. He volunteered no word on their way thither, but lay back among his cushions and pillows with closed eyes, pale and exhausted—though the doctors assured the Maxwells that there was no cause for anxiety on the score of his removal, when they urged that he be left in their care until he had regained more strength.

It was a white and scared Virginia who listened to Hepsey's account of all that had happened—an account which neither over-stated the Bascoms' debt to the Maxwells nor spared Virginia's guilty conscience.

When she found that her father had been the guest of the Maxwells and that they had played the part of good Samaritans to him in the tent in which the Senior Warden had obliged them to take refuge, she was thoroughly mortified, and there was a struggle between false pride and proper gratitude.

"It is very awkward, is it not, Mrs. Burke?" she said. "I ought certainly to call on Mrs. Maxwell and thank her—but—under the circumstances—"

"What circumstances?" asked Hepsey.

"Well, you know, it will be very embarrassing for me to go to Mr. Maxwell's tent after what has happened between him and—my father."

"I'm not sure that I catch on, Virginia. Which happenin' do you mean? Your father's cold-blooded ejection of the Maxwells from their house, or Mr. Maxwell's warm-blooded sacrifice to save your father's life? Perhaps it *is* a bit embarrassing, as you call it, to thank a man for givin' his blood to save your father."

"It is a more personal matter than that," replied Virginia, gazing dramatically out of the window. "You don't quite seem to appreciate the delicacy of the situation, Mrs. Burke."

"No, I'm blessed if I do. But then you know I'm very stupid about some things, Virginia. Fact is, I'm just stupid enough to imagine—no, I mean think—that it would be the most natural thing in the world to go straight to the Maxwells and thank 'em for all they've done for your father in takin' him in and givin' him the kind of care that money can't buy. There's special reasons that I needn't mention why you should say thank you, and say it right."

Virginia examined the toe of her boot for some time in silence and then began:

"But you don't understand the situation, Mrs. Burke."

"Virginia, if you don't stop that kind of thing, I shall certainly send for the police. Are you *lookin'* for a situation? If you have got anything to say, say it."

"Well, to be quite frank with you, Mrs. Burke, I must confess that at one time Mr. Maxwell and I were supposed to be very good friends."

"Naturally. You ought to be good friends with your rector. I don't see anything tragic about that."

"But we were something more than friends."

"Who told you? You can't believe all you hear in a town like this. Maybe some one was foolin' you."

"I ought to know what I am talking about. He accepted our hospitality at Willow Bluff, and was so attentive that people began to make remarks."

"Well, people have been makin' remarks ever since Eve told Adam to put his apron on for dinner. Any fool can make remarks, and the biggest fool is the one who cares. Are you sure that you didn't make any remarks yourself, Virginia?"

Virginia instantly bridled, and looked the picture of injured innocence.

"Certainly not!" she retorted. "Do you think that I would talk about such a delicate matter before others?"

"Oh no; I suppose not. But you could look wise and foolish at the same time when Maxwell's name was mentioned, with a coy and kittenish air which would suggest more than ten volumes of Mary Jane Holmes."

"You are not very sympathetic, Mrs. Burke, when I am in deep trouble. I want your help, not ridicule and abuse."

"Well, I am sorry for you, Virginia, in more ways than one. But really I'd like to know what reason you have to think that Donald Maxwell was ever in love with you; I suppose that's what you mean."

Virginia blushed deeply, as became a gentle maiden of her tender years, and replied:

"Oh, it is not a question of things which one can easily define. Love is vocal without words, you know."

"Hm! You don't mean that he made love to you and proposed to you through a phonograph? You know I had some sort of idea that love that was all wool, and a yard wide, and meant business, usually got vocal at times."

"But Mr. Maxwell and I were thrown together in such an intimate way in parish work, you know."

"Which did the throwing?"

"You don't for one moment suppose that I would intrude myself, or press myself on his attention, do you?"

"Oh my gracious, no! He is not the kind of a man to be easily impressed. He may have seen a girl or two before he met you; of course I mean just incidentally, as it were. Now, Virginia Bascom, allow me to ask you one or two plain questions. Did he ever ask you to marry him?"

"No, not in so many words."

"Did he ever give you any plain indication that he wanted to marry you? Did he ever play the mandolin under your window at midnight? Did he ever steal one of your gloves, or beg for a rose out of your bouquet, or turn the gas out when he called?"

"No, but one night he sat on the sofa with me and told me that I was a great assistance to him in his parish work, and that he felt greatly indebted to me."

"Hm! That's certainly rather pronounced, isn't it? Did you call your father, or rise hastily and leave the room, or what did you do?"

"Well, of course it was not a proposal, but the way he did it was very suggestive, and calculated to give a wrong impression, especially as he had his arm on the back of the sofa behind me."

"Maybe he was makin' love to the sofa. Didn't you know that Donald Maxwell was engaged to be married before he ever set foot in Durford?"

"Good gracious, no! What are you talking about?"

"Well, he certainly was, for keeps."

"Then he had no business to pose as a free man, if he were engaged. It is dreadful to have to lose faith in one's rector. It is next to losing faith in—in—"

"The milk-man. Yes, I quite agree with you. But you see I don't recall that Donald Maxwell did any posing. He simply kept quiet about his own affairs—though I do think that it would have been better to let people know that he was engaged, from the start. However, he may have concluded his private affairs were his own business. I know that's very stupid; but some people will persist in doin' it, in spite of all you can say to 'em. Perhaps it never occurred to him that he would be expected to marry anyone living in a little sawed-off settlement like this."

"There's no use in abusing your native village; and"—her voice quavered on the verge of tears—"I think you are very unsympathetic." She buried her nose in her handkerchief.

Mrs. Burke gazed sternly at Virginia for a full minute and then inquired:

"Well, do you want to know why? You started with just foolishness, but you've ended up with meanness, Virginia Bascom. You've taken your revenge on people who've done you nothin' but kindness. I know pretty well who it was that suggested to your father that the mortgage on the rectory should be foreclosed, and the Maxwells turned out of house and home. He's always been close-fisted, but I've never known him to be dead ugly and vindictive before.

"Yes. You were behind all this wretched business—and you're sorry for it, and wish you could undo the unkindness you've done. Now I am goin' to talk business—better than talkin' sympathy, because it'll make you feel better when you've done what I tell you. You go and call on Mrs. Betty immediately, and tell her that you are very grateful to her husband for saving your father's life, and that money couldn't possibly pay for the things she and Mr. Maxwell did for him, and that you're everlastingly indebted to 'em both."

"But—but," wailed the repentant Virginia, "what can I say about the tent? Pa won't go back on that—not if his life had been saved twice over."

"Never you mind about that. You do your part of the business, and leave the rest to the other feller. You can bet your bottom dollar it won't be the Maxwells that'll raise the question of who turned 'em out of the rectory."

"I'll go right away, before I weaken. Oh," she cried, as Hepsey put a strengthening arm about her, "I've been wrong—I know I have. However shall I make it right again?"

When Virginia arrived at the tent and pulled the bell-cord, Mrs. Betty pushed apart the curtains and greeted her visitor with the utmost cordiality.

"Oh, Miss Bascom! I am *so* glad to see you. Come right in. Donald is out just now; but he will return presently, and I'm sure will be delighted to see an old friend. This way, please. Is your father improving satisfactorily?"

This greeting was so utterly different from what she had expected, that for the moment she was silent; but when they were seated she began:

"Mrs. Maxwell, I don't know how to express my gratitude to you for all you have done for my father. I—I—"

"Then I wouldn't try, Miss Bascom. Don't give the matter a single thought. We were glad to do what we could for your father, and we made him as comfortable as we could."

Virginia's heart was quite atrophied, and so with choking voice she began:

"And I'm afraid that I have not been very civil to you—in fact, I am sure that I owe you an apology—"

"No, never mind. It's all right now. Suppose you take off your things and stay to supper with us. Then we can have a real good visit, and you will see how well we dwellers in tents can live!"

Virginia winced; but for some reason which she could not understand she found it quite impossible to decline the invitation.

"I'm sure you are very kind, Mrs. Maxwell; but I'm afraid I shall inconvenience you."

"Oh no, not a bit. Now will you be a real good Samaritan and help me a little, as I have no maid? You might set the table if you don't mind, and when Donald comes we shall be ready for him. This is really quite jolly," she added, bustling about, showing Virginia where to find things.

"I am afraid," Virginia began with something like a sob in her voice, "that you are heaping coals of fire on my head."

"Oh no; not when coal is over seven dollars a ton. We couldn't afford such extravagant hospitality as that. You might arrange those carnations in the vase if you will, while I attend to the cooking. You will find the china, and the silver, in that chest. I won't apologize for the primitive character of our entertainment because you see when we came down here we stored most of our things in Mrs. Burke's barn. It is awfully nice to have somebody with me; I am so much alone; you came just in time to save me from the blues."

When Mrs. Betty disappeared in the "kitchen," and Virginia began the task assigned her, a very queer and not altogether pleasant sensation filled her heart. Was it remorse, or penitence, or self-reproach, or indigestion? She could not be absolutely sure about it, but concluded that perhaps it was a combination of all four. When Donald returned, and discovered Virginia trying to decide whether they would need two spoons or three at each plate, for an instant he was too astonished to speak; but quickly regaining his easy manner, he welcomed her no less cordially than Mrs. Betty had done, remarking:

"Well, this is a treat; and so you are going to have supper with us? That will be a great pleasure."

Virginia almost collapsed in momentary embarrassment, and could think of nothing better than to ask:

"I am not sure what Mrs. Maxwell is going to have for supper, and I really don't know whether to place two spoons or three. What would you advise, Mr. Maxwell?"

Maxwell scowled seriously, rubbed his chin and replied:

"Well, you know, I really can't say; but perhaps it would be on the safe side to have three spoons in case any emergency might arise, like a custard, or jelly and whipped cream, or something else which Betty likes to make as a surprise. Yes, on the whole, I think that three would be better than two."

When Virginia had placed the spoons, and Maxwell had returned to assist her, she hesitated a moment and looked at him with tears in her eyes and began:

"Mr. Maxwell, there is something I must say to you, an acknowledgment and an apology I must make. I have been so horribly—"

"Now see here, Miss Virginia," the rector replied, "you just forget it. We are awfully glad to have you here, and we are going to have a right jolly supper together. Betty's muffins are simply fine, and her creamed chicken is a dream. Besides, I want to consult you concerning the new wardrobe I am going to have built in the vestry. You see there is the question of the drawers, and the shelves, and—"

"Never mind the drawers and the shelves," Mrs. Betty remarked as she entered with the creamed chicken and the muffins. "You just sit down before these things get cold, and you can talk business afterwards."

To her utter astonishment Virginia soon found herself eating heartily, utterly at her ease in the cordial, friendly atmosphere of tent-life, and when Maxwell took her home later in the evening, she hadn't apologized or wallowed in an agony of self-reproach. She had only demanded the recipe for the muffins, and had declared that she was coming again very soon if Mrs. Betty would only let her.

And last but not least—the rector's polite attention in acting as her escort home failed to work upon her dramatic temperament with any more startling effect than to produce a feeling that he was a very good friend.

In fact, she wondered, as she conned over the events of the evening, whether she had realized before, all that the word *Friendship* signified.

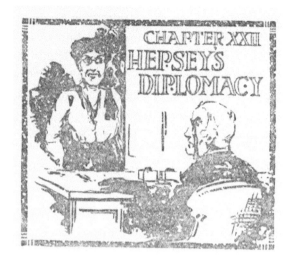

"I don't rightly know what's got into Virginia Bascom," remarked Jonathan, as he sat on Hepsey's side porch one evening, making polite conversation as his new habit was. "She's buzzin' round Mrs. Betty like a bee round a flower — thicker'n thieves they be, by gum."

"Yes," cogitated Hepsey, half to herself, and half in response, "the lamb's lyin' down all right, and it's about time we'd got the lion curled up by her and purrin' like a cat. But I don't see the signs of it, and I'll have to take my knittin' to-morrow and sit right down in his den and visit with him a little. If he won't purr, I've got what'll make him roar, good and proper, or I've missed my guess."

"Now Hepsey, you go easy with my church-partner, the Senior Warden. When his wife lived, he was a decent sort of a feller, was Sylvester Bascom; and I reckon she got him comin' her way more with molasses than with vinegar."

And though Hepsey snorted contempt for the advice of a mere male, she found the thought top-side of her mind as she started out next morning to pay Bascom a momentous call. After all, Jonathan had but echoed her own consistent philosophy of life. But with her usual shrewdness she decided to go armed with both kinds of ammunition.

Mrs. Burke puffed somewhat loudly as she paused on the landing which led to the door of Bascom's office. After wiping her forehead with her handkerchief she gave three loud knocks on the painted glass of the door, which shook some of the loose putty onto the floor. After knocking the third time some one called out "Come in," and she opened the door, entered, and gazed calmly across the room. Bascom was seated at his desk talking to a farmer, and when he turned around and discovered who his visitor was, he ejaculated irreverently:

"Good Lord deliver us!"

"Oh, do excuse me!" Mrs. Burke replied. "I didn't know that you were sayin' the Litany. I'll just slip into the next room and wait till you get through."

Whereupon she stepped into the next room, closed the door, and made herself comfortable in a large arm-chair. There was a long table in the middle of the room, and the walls were covered with shelves and yellow books of a most monotonous binding. The air was musty and close. She quietly opened one of the windows, and having resumed her seat, she pulled a wash-rag from her leather bag and began knitting calmly.

She waited for some time, occasionally glancing at the long table, which was covered with what appeared to be a hopeless confusion of letters, legal documents, and books opened and turned face downward. Occasionally she sniffed in disgust at the general untidiness of the place. Evidently the appearance of the table in front of her was getting on her nerves; and so she put her knitting away as she muttered to herself:

"I wonder Virginia don't come up here once in a while and put things to rights. It's simply awful!" Then she began sorting the papers and gathering them into little uniform piles by themselves. She seemed to have no notion whatever of their possible relation to each other, but arranged them according to their size and color in nice little separate piles. When there was nothing else left for her to do she resumed her knitting and waited patiently for the departure of the farmer. The two men seemed to be having a rather warm dispute over the interpretation of some legal contract; and if Bascom was hot-tempered and emphatic in his language, bordering on the profane, the client was stubborn and dull-witted and hard to convince. Occasionally she overheard bits of the controversy which were not intended for her ears. Bascom insisted:

"But you're not such a dum fool as to think that a contract legally made between two parties is not binding, are you? You admit that I have fulfilled my part, and now you must pay for the services rendered or else I shall bring suit against you."

The reply to this was not audible, but the farmer did not seem to be quite convinced.

After what seemed to her an interminable interval the door banged, and she knew that Bascom was alone. She did not wait for any invitation, but rising quietly she went into the inner office and took the chair vacated by the farmer. Bascom made a pretense of writing, in silence, with his back towards her, during which interval Hepsey waited patiently. Then, looking up with the expression of a deaf-mute, he asked colorlessly:

"Well, Mrs. Burke, what may I do for you?"

"You can do nothing for me—but you can and must do something for the Maxwells," she replied firmly but quietly.

"Don't you think it would be better to let Maxwell take care of his own affairs?"

"Yes, most certainly, if he were in a position to do so. But you know that the clergy are a long-sufferin' lot, more's the pity; they'll endure almost anythin' rather than complain. That's why you and others take advantage of them."

"Ah, but an earnest minister of the Gospel does not look for the loaves and fishes of his calling."

"I shouldn't think he would. I hate fish, myself; but Maxwell has a perfect right to look for the honest fulfillment of a contract made between you and him. Didn't I hear you tell that farmer that he was a dum fool if he thought that a contract made between two parties is not legally binding, and that if you fulfilled your part he must pay for your services or you would sue him? Do you suppose that a contract with a carpenter or a plumber or a mason is binding, while a contract with a clergyman is not? What is the matter with you, anyway?"

Bascom made no reply, but turned his back towards Hepsey and started to write. She resumed:

"Donald Maxwell's salary is goin' to be paid him in full within the next two weeks or—"

Mrs. Burke came to a sudden silence, and after a moment or two Bascom turned around and inquired sarcastically:

"Or what?"

Hepsey continued to knit in silence for a while, her face working in her effort to gain control of herself and speak calmly.

"Now see here, Sylvester Bascom: I didn't come here to have a scene with you, and if I knit like I was fussed, you must excuse me."

Her needles had been flashing lightning, and truth to tell, Bascom, for all he dreaded Hepsey's sharp tongue as nothing else in Durford, had been unable to keep his eyes off those angry bits of sparkling steel. Suddenly they stopped—dead. The knitting fell into Hepsey's lap, and she sat forward—a pair of kindly, moist eyes searching the depths of Bascom's, as he looked up at her. Her voice dropped to a lower tone as she continued:

"There's been just one person, and one person only, that's ever been able to keep the best of you on top—and she was my best friend, your wife. She kept you human, and turned even the worst side of you to some account. If you did scrape and grub, 'most night and day, to make your pile, and was hard on those that crossed your path while doin' of it, it was she that showed you there was pleasure in usin' it for others as well as for yourself, and while she lived you did it. But since she's been gone,"—the old man tried to keep his face firm and his glance steady, but in vain—he winced,—"since she's been gone, the human in you's dried up like a sun-baked apple. And it's you, Sylvester Bascom, that's been made the most miserable, 'spite of all the little carks you've put on many another."

His face hardened again, and Hepsey paused.

"What has all this to do with Mr. Maxwell, may I ask?"

"I'm comin' to that," continued Hepsey, patiently. "If Mary Bascom were alive to-day, would the rector of Durford be livin' in a tent instead of in the rectory—the house she thought she had given over, without mortgage or anything else, to the church? And would you be holdin' back your subscription to the church, and seein' that others held back too? I never thought you'd have done, when she was dead, what'd have broken her heart if she'd been livin'. The church was her one great interest in life, after her husband and her daughter; and it was *her* good work that brought the parish to make you Senior Warden. After you'd made money and moved to your new house, just before she died, she gave the old house, that was hers from her father, to the church, and you were to make the legal transfer of it. Then she died suddenly, and you delayed and delayed—claiming the house as yours, and at last sold it to us subject to the mortgage."

The old man stirred uneasily in his chair.

"This is all quite beside the mark. What might have been proper to do in my wife's life-time became a different matter altogether after her death. I had my daughter's welfare to think of; besides—"

"I'm not talkin' about your legal right. But you know that if you'd wanted to have it, you could have got your interest on the mortgage quick enough. If you hadn't held back on his salary, others wouldn't have; or if they had, you could have got after 'em. What's the use of tryin' to mix each other up? You couldn't keep Maxwell in your pocket, and because he didn't come to you every day for orders you reckoned to turn him out of the parish. You've not one thing against him, and you know it, Sylvester Bascom. He's shown you every kind of respect as his Senior Warden, and more patience than you deserved. He let himself be—no, *had* himself—bled, to save your life. But instead of making him the best young friend you could have had, and makin' yourself of real use to your town and your neighbors through him and his work, you've let the devil get into you; and when your accident come, you'd got to where you were runnin' that fast down a steep place into the sea that I could 'most hear the splash."

She cocked her head on one side, and smiled at him whimsically, hoping for some response to her humorous picture. A faint ghost of a smile—was it, or was it not?—flickered on the old man's lips; but he gave no sign of grace.

Hepsey sighed, and paused for an instant. "Well—we can't sit here talkin' till midnight, or I shall be compromisin' your reputation, I suppose. There'll be a meeting of the parishioners called at the end of this week, and the rector won't be present at it; so, Warden, I suppose you'll preside. I hope you will. I've got to do my part—and that is to see that the parish understands just how their rector's placed, right now, both about his house and his salary. He's workin' as a laborer to get enough for him and that little wife of his to live on, and the town knows it—but they don't all know that it's because the salary that's properly his is bein' held back on him, and by those that pay their chauffeurs more than the rector gets, by a good piece. I shall call on every one at that meetin' to pay up; and I shall begin with the poorest, and end up"—she fixed Bascom's eye, significantly—"with the richest. And if it seems to be my duty to do it, I may have somethin' more to say when the subscription's closed—but I don't believe—no," she added, opening her bag and rummaging about among its contents till she hit upon a letter and brought it forth, "no, I don't believe I'll have to say a thing. I've got a hunch, Sylvester Bascom, that it'll be you that'll have the last word, after all."

"I'VE GOT A HUNCH, SYLVESTER BASCOM, THAT IT'LL BE
YOU THAT'LL HAVE THE LAST WORD, AFTER ALL"

The old man's glance was riveted upon the familiar handwriting of
the faded letter, and without a word Hepsey started to read it, date
and all, in a clear voice:

WILLOW BLUFF, DURFORD.
September —, 19—.

HEPSEY DEAR:

I suppose you will never forgive me for making the move from the
old house to Willow Bluff, as it's to be called, while you were not
home to help me. But they got finished sooner than we thought for,
and Sylvester was as eager as a child with a new toy to get moved
in. So here we are, and the first letter I write from our new home is to
you, who helped more than anyone to make the old home happy for
me and mine—bless them and bless you!

Everything is out of the old house—"The Rectory" as I shall call it,
now—except such pieces of furniture as we did not want to take
away, and we thought might be welcome to the parson (or parsons, I
suppose) who may occupy it. Sister Susan thought it slighting to Pa's
generosity to give the house to the church; but I don't look at it like

that. Anyway, it's done now—and I'm very happy to think that the flock can offer a proper home to its shepherd, as long as the old place stands.

If you get back Thursday I shall just be ready for you to help me with the shades and curtains, if you care to.

Your friend,
MARION ANDERSON BASCOM.

P. S. Ginty sends her love to Aunt Hepsey, and says, "to come to Boston quick!" She's a little confused, someway, and can't get it out of her head that we're not back home in Boston, since we left the old place. I hope you are having a nice visit with Sally.

As Hepsey read, Sylvester Bascom turned, slowly, away from her, his head on his hand, gazing out of the window. When she had finished reading, the letter was folded up and replaced in the bag along with her knitting. Then, laying her hand with a gentle, firm pressure on the old man's shoulder, Mrs. Burke departed.

CHAPTER XXII

HEPSEY CALLS
A MEETING

For the next few days Hepsey's mind worked in unfamiliar channels, for her nature was that of a benevolent autocrat, and she had found herself led by circumstances into a situation demanding the prowess and elasticity of the diplomat. To begin with, she must risk a gamble at the meeting: if the spiritual yeast did not rise in old Bascom, as she hoped it would, and crown her strategy with success, she would have to fall back on belligerent tactics, and see if it were not possible to get his duty out of him by threatened force of public opinion: and she knew that, with his obstinacy, it would be touch and go on which side of the fence he would fall in a situation of that kind — dependent, in fact, upon the half turn of a screw, more or less, for the result. Furthermore, she concluded that beyond the vaguest hint of her call on Bascom and the object of the meeting, she could not show her hand to Maxwell; for he would feel it his duty to step in and prevent the possibility of any such open breach as failure on Hepsey's part would probably make in the parish solidarity. For once she must keep her own counsel—except for Jonathan, whose present infatuated condition made him an even safer and more satisfactory source of "advice" than he normally was. But the evening before the meeting, as he sat on Hepsey's porch, he began to experience qualms, perhaps in his capacity as Junior Warden. But Hepsey turned upon him relentlessly:

"Now see here! You know I don't start somethin' unless I can see it through; and if it means a scrap, so much the better. Next to a good revival, a good hard scrap in a stupid parish has a real spiritual value. It stimulates the circulation, increases the appetite, gives people somethin' to think about, and does a lot of good where peaceful ways would fail. The trouble with us is that we've always been a sight too peaceful. If I've got to do it, I'm goin' to make a row, a real jolly row that'll make some people wish they'd never been born. No-no-no! Don't you try to interfere. We've come to a crisis, and I'm goin' to meet it. Don't you worry until I begin to holler for first aid to the injured. A woman can't vote for a vestryman, though women form the bulk of the congregation, and do most all of the parish work; and the whole church'd go to smithereens if it weren't for the women. But there's one thing a woman can always do: *She can talk*. They say that talk is cheap; but sometimes it's a mighty expensive article, if it's the right kind; and maybe the men will have to settle the bills. I'm going to *talk*; perhaps you think that's nothing new. But you don't know how I can talk when once I get my dander up. Somebody's goin' to sit up and pay attention this time. Bascom'll conclude to preside at the meetin'; whichever way he means to act; and I've fixed it so Maxwell will be engaged on other duties. No; go 'way. I don't want to see you around here again until the whole thing's over."

"All right Hepsey, all right. I guess if it goes through the way you want you'll be that set up you'll be wantin' to marry old Bascom 'stead of me," chuckled Jonathan, as the lady of his choice turned to enter the house.

She faced round upon him as she reached the door, her features set with grim determination:

"If I get the whole caboodle, bag and baggage, from the meetin' and from Bascom, there's no knowin' but what I'll send for the parson and be married right there and then. There isn't a thing I could think of, in the line of a real expensive sacrifice, that'd measure up as compensation for winnin' out—not even marryin' you, Jonathan Jackson."

So Hepsey laid down lines for control of the meeting, ready with a different variety of expedients, from point to point in its progress, as Sylvester Bascom's attitude at the time might necessitate. For she felt very little anxiety as to her ability to carry the main body of the audience along with her.

The night of the meeting the Sunday School Room, adjacent to the church, was filled full to a seat at least a quarter of an hour before the time announced for the meeting. Hepsey had provided herself with a chair in the center of the front row, directly facing the low platform to be occupied by the chairman. Her leather bag hung formidably on one arm, and a long narrow blank book was laid on her lap. She took little notice of her surroundings, and her anxiety was imperceptible, as she thrummed with a pencil upon the book, glancing now and then at the side door, watching for Bascom's entrance. The meeting buzzed light conversation, as a preliminary. Had she miscalculated on the very first move? Was he going to treat the whole affair with lofty disdain? As the hour struck, dead silence reigned in the room, expectant; and Jonathan, who sat next her, fidgeted nervously.

"Five minutes' grace, and that's all; if he's not here by then, it'll be up to you to call the meetin' to order," whispered Hepsey.

"Sakes!" hissed the terrified Junior Warden, "you didn't say nothin' about that, Hepsey," he protested.

She leveled a withering glance at him, and was about to reduce him to utter impotence by some scathing remark, when both were startled by a voice in front of them, issuing from "the chair." Silently the Senior Warden had entered, and had proceeded to open the meeting. His face was set and stern, and his voice hard and toneless. No help from that quarter, Hepsey mentally recorded.

"As the rector of this parish is not able to be present I have been asked to preside at this meeting. I believe that it was instigated—that is suggested, by some of the ladies who believe that there are some matters of importance which need immediate attention, and must be presented to the congregation without delay. I must beg to remind these ladies that the Wardens and Vestrymen are the business officers of the church; and it seems to my poor judgment that if any business is to be transacted, the proper way would be for the Vestry to take care of it. However, I have complied with the request and have undertaken to preside, in the absence of the rector. The meeting is now open for business."

Bascom sat down and gazed at the audience, but with a stare so expressionless as gave no further index to his mood. For some time there was a rather painful silence; but at last Hepsey Burke arose and faced about to command the audience.

"Brethren and sisters," she began, "a few of us women have made up our minds that it's high time that somethin' was done towards payin' our rector what we owe him, and that we furnish him with a proper house to live in."

At this point, a faint murmur of applause interrupted the speaker, who replied: "There. There. Don't be too quick. You won't feel a bit like applaudin' when I get through. It's a burnin' shame and disgrace that we owe Mr. Maxwell about two hundred dollars, which means a mighty lot to him, because if he was paid in full every month he would get just about enough to keep his wife and himself from starvin' to death. I wasn't asked to call this meetin'; I asked the rector to, and I asked the Senior Warden to preside. And I told the rector that some of us—both men and women—had business to talk about that wasn't for his ears. For all he knows, we're here to pass a vote of censure on him. The fact is that we have reached the point where somethin' has got to be done right off quick; and if none of the Vestrymen do it, then a poor shrinkin' little woman like myself has got to rise and mount the band wagon. I'm no woman's rights woman, but I have a conscience that'll keep me awake nights until I have freed my mind."

Here Hepsey paused, and twirling her pencil between her lips, gazed around at her auditors who were listening with breathless attention. Then she suddenly exclaimed with suppressed wrath, and in her penetrating tones:

"What is the matter with you men, anyway? You'd have to pay your butcher, or your baker, or your grocer, whether you wanted to or not. Then why in the name of conscience don't you pay your parson?

Certainly religion that don't cost nothin' is worse than nothin'. I'll tell you the reason why you don't support your parson: It's just because your rector's a gentleman, and can't very well kick over the traces, or balk, or sue you, even if you do starve him. So you, prosperous, big-headed men think that you can sneak out of it. Oh, you needn't shuffle and look mad; you're goin' to get the truth for once, and I had Johnny Mullins lock the front door before I began."

The whole audience responded to this sally with a laugh, but the speaker relented not one iota. "Then when you've smit your rector on one cheek you quote the Bible to make him think he ought to turn his overcoat also." Another roar. "There: you don't need to think I'm havin' a game. I'm not through yet. Now let's get right down to business. We owe our rector a lot of money, and he is livin' in a tent because we neglected to pay the interest on the rectory mortgage held by the Senior Warden of our church. Talkin' plain business, and nothin' else, turned him out of house and home, and we broke our business contract with him. Yes we did! And now you know it.

"Some of us have been sayin'—and I was one of 'em till Mr. Maxwell corrected me—that it was mean of Mr. Bascom to turn the rector and his wife out of their house. But business is business, and until we've paid the last cent of our contributions, we haven't any right to throw stones at anyone. Wait till we've done our part, for that! We've been the laughing stock of the whole town because of our pesky meanness. That tent of ours has stuck out on the landscape like a horse fly on a pillow sham.

"It's not my business to tell how the rector and his wife have had to economize and suffer, to get along at all; or how nice and uncomplainin' they've been through it all. They wouldn't want me to say anythin' of that; sportsmen they are, both of 'em. The price of food's gone up, and the rector's salary gone down like a teeter on a log.

"Now, as I remarked before, let's get right down to business. The only way to raise that money is to raise it! There's no use larkin' all 'round Robin Hood's barn, or scampering round the mulberry bush any longer. I don't care for fairs myself, where you have to go and buy somethin' you don't want, for five times what it's worth, and call it givin' to the Lord. And I don't care to give a chicken, and then have to pay for eatin' the same old bird afterwards. I won't eat soda biscuit unless I know who made 'em. Church fairs are an invention of the devil to make people think they're religious, when they are only mighty restless and selfish.

"The only thing to do is to put your hands in your trousers pockets and pay, cash down, just as you would in any business transaction. And by cash, I don't mean five cents in the plate Sunday, and a dollar for a show on Tuesday. We've none of us any business to pretend to give to the Lord what doesn't cost a red cent, as the Bible says, somewheres. Now don't get nervous. I'm going to start a subscription paper right here and now. It'll save lots of trouble, and you ought to jump at the chance. You'll be votin' me a plated ice-water pitcher before we get through, for bein' so good to you—just as a little souvenir of the evenin'."

A disjointed murmur of disapproval rose from sundry parts of the room at this summary way of meeting the emergency. Nelson, who had tried in vain to catch the eye of the chair, rose at a venture and remarked truculently:

"This is a most unusual proceeding, Mrs. Burke."

The chair remained immobile—but Hepsey turned upon the foe like a flash of lightning.

"Precisely, Mr. Nelson. And we are a most unusual parish. I don't claim to have any information gained by world-wide travel, but livin' my life as I've found it here, in ths town, I've got to say, that this is the first time I ever heard of a church turnin' its rector out of house and home, and refusin' to give him salary enough to buy food for his family. Maybe in the course of your professional travels this thing has got to be an everyday occurrence to you,—but there's some of us here, that 'aint got much interest in such goings-on, outside of Durford."

"You have no authority to raise money for the church; I believe the Warden will concur in that opinion?" and he bowed towards Bascom.

"That is a point for the meeting to decide," he replied judicially, as Hepsey turned towards him.

"Seems to me," continued Mrs. Burke, facing the audience, "that authority won't fill the rector's purse so well as cash. It's awful curious how a church with six Vestrymen and two Wardens, all of them good business men—men that can squeeze money out of a monkey-wrench, and always get the best of the other fellow in a horse-trade, and smoke cigars enough to pay the rector's whole salary—get limp and faint and find it necessary to fall back on talkin' about 'authority' when any money is to be raised. What we want in the parish is not authority, but just everyday plain business hustle, the sort of hustle that wears trousers; and as we don't seem to get that, the next best kind is the sort that wears skirts. I'd always rather that men shall do the public work than women; but if men won't, women must. What we need right here in Durford is a few full grown men who aren't shirks or quitters, who can put up prayers with one hand while they put down the cash with the other; and I don't believe the Lord ever laid it up against any man who paid first, and prayed afterwards.

"Now brethren, don't all speak at once. I'm goin' to start takin' subscriptions. Who's goin' to head the list?"

A little withered old woman laboriously struggled to her feet, and in a high-pitched, quavering voice began:

"I'd like to give suthin' towards the end in view. Our rector were powerful good to my Thomas when he had the brown kitties in his throat. He came to see him mos' every day and read to him, and said prayers with him, and brought him papers and jelly. He certainly were powerful good to my Thomas; and once when Thomas had a fever our rector said that he thought that a bath would do my Thomas a heap of good, and he guessed he'd give him one. So I got some water in a bowl and some soap, and our rector he just took off his coat, and his vest, and his collar, and his cuffs, and our rector he washed Thomas, and he washed him, and he wa—"

"Well," Hepsey interrupted, to stay the flow of eloquence, "so you'd like to pay for his laundry now, would you Mrs. Sumner? Shall I put you down for two dollars? Good! Mrs. Sumner sets the ball rollin' with two dollars. Who'll be the next?"

As there was no response, Mrs. Burke glanced critically over the assembly until she had picked her man, and then announced:

"Hiram Mason, I'm sure you must be on the anxious bench?"

Hiram colored painfully as he replied:

"I don't know as I am prepared to say what I can give, just at present, Mrs. Burke."

"Well now let's think about it a little. Last night's *Daily Bugle* had your name in a list of those that gave ten dollars apiece at St. Bridget's fair. I suppose the Irish trade's valuable to a grocer like yourself; but you surely can't do less for your own church? I'll put you down for ten, though of course you can double it if you like."

"No," said Hiram, meditatively; "I guess ten'll do."

"Hiram Mason gives ten dollars. The Lord loveth a cheerful giver. Thanks, Hiram."

Again there was a pause; and as no one volunteered, Hepsey continued:

"Sylvester Perkins, how much will you give?"

"I suppose I'll give five dollars," Sylvester responded, before Mrs. Burke could have a chance to put him down for a larger sum. "But I don't like this way of doin' things a little bit. It's not a woman's place to hold up a man and rob him in public meetin'."

"No, a woman usually goes through her husband's pockets when he's asleep, I suppose. But you see I'm not your wife. Thanks, Mr. Perkins: Mr. Perkins, *five* dollars," she repeated as she entered his subscription in the book. "Next?" she called briskly.

"Mrs. Burke, I'll give twenty dollars, if you think that's enough," called a voice from the back timidly.

Everyone turned to the speaker in some surprise. He was a delicate, slender fellow, evidently in bad health. He trembled nervously, and Mrs. Burke hesitated for an instant, between fear of hurting his feelings and letting him give more than she knew he could possibly afford.

"I am afraid you ought not to give so much, Amos. Let me put you down for five," she said kindly. "We mustn't rob Peter to pay Paul."

"No, ma'am, put me down for twenty," he persisted; and then burst forth—"and I wish it was twenty thousand. I'd do anything for Mr. Maxwell; I owe it to him, I tell you."

The speaker hesitated a moment and wiped his forehead with his handkerchief, and then continued slowly, and with obvious effort:

"Maybe you'll think I am a fool to give myself away before a crowd like this, and I a member of the church; but the simple fact is that Mr. Maxwell saved my life once, when I was pretty near all in."

Again the speaker stopped, breathing heavily, and there was absolute silence in the room. Regaining his courage, he continued: "Yes, he saved me, body and soul, and I guess I'll tell the whole story. Most of you would have kicked me into the street or lodged me in jail; but he wasn't that kind, thank God!

"I was clerking in the Post Office a while back, and I left town one night, suddenly. I'd been drinking some, and when I left, my accounts were two hundred dollars short. The thing was kept quiet. Only two men knew about it. Mr. Maxwell was one. He got the other man to keep his mouth shut, handed over the amount, and chased after me and made me come back with him and stay at his house for a while. Then he gave me some work and helped me to make a new start. He didn't say a word of reproach, nor he didn't talk religion to me. He just acted as if he cared a whole lot for me, and wanted to put me on my feet again.

"I didn't know for a long time where Mr. Maxwell got the money for me but after a while I discovered that he'd given a chattel mortgage on his books and personal belongings. Do you suppose that there's anybody else in the world would have done that for me?

It wasn't only his giving me the money; it was finding that somebody trusted me and cared for me, who had no business to trust me, and couldn't afford to trust me. That's what saved me and kept me straight.

"I haven't touched a drop since, and I never will. I've been paying my debt to him as quick as I can, and as far as money can pay it; but all the gold in the world wouldn't even me up with him. I don't know just why I've told all about it, but I guess it's because I felt you ought to know the kind of a man the rector is; and I'm glad he isn't here, or he'd never have let me give him away like this."

Amos sat down, while the astonished gathering stared at him, the defaulter, who in a moment of gratitude had betrayed himself. The woman next to him edged a little farther away from him and watched him furtively, but he did not seem to care.

Under the stimulus of this confession, the feelings of the people quickly responded to the occasion, and a line soon formed, without further need of wit or eloquence on Hepsey's part, to have their subscriptions recorded. In half an hour, Mrs. Burke, whose face was glowing with pleasure—albeit she glanced anxiously from time to time towards old Mr. Bascom, in an endeavor to size up his mood and force his intentions—had written down the name of the last volunteer. She turned towards her audience:

"As I don't want to keep you waitin' here all night while I add up the subscriptions, I'll ask the chairman to do it for me and let you know the result. He's quicker at figurin' than I am, I guess," with which compliment, she smilingly handed the book to the Senior Warden. While the old man bent to his task, the room buzzed with low, excited conversation. Enough was already known of Bascom's hostility to the rector, to make the meeting decidedly curious as to his attitude towards Hepsey's remarks and the mortgage; and they knew him well enough to be aware that he would not allow that item in her speech to go unanswered, in some way or other.

All eyes rested upon the gaunt figure of the chairman, as he rose to his feet to announce the total of the subscription list. He cleared his throat, and looked down at Hepsey Burke; and Jonathan, as he squinted anxiously at Hepsey by his side, noticed that she sat with her eyes tight-closed, oblivious of the chairman's glance. Jonathan looked hastily up at Bascom, and noticed him shift his position a little nervously, as he cleared his throat again.

"The amount subscribed on this list, is two hundred and thirty-seven dollars and thirty-five cents," he said. The loud applause was instantaneous, and Jonathan turned quickly to Hepsey, as he stamped his feet and clapped his hands.

"Thirty-seven thirty-five more than we owe him; Hepsey, you've done fine," he chortled.

But Hepsey's look was now riveted on the chairman, and except for a half-absent smile of pleasure, the keenest anxiety showed in her expression.

Bascom cleared his voice again, and then proceeded:

"Mrs. Burke informed you that the rector's salary was in arrears to the extent of about two hundred dollars. It is now for this meeting to pass a formal resolution for the application of the amount subscribed to the object in view."

Hepsey's lips narrowed; not a cent was down on the list to the name of the Senior Warden; the debt was being paid without assistance from him.

"I presume I may put it to the meeting that the amount, when collected, be paid over to the rector by a committee formed for that purpose?" proceeded the chairman.

This resolution being duly seconded and carried, Bascom continued:

"Before we adjourn I request the opportunity to make a few remarks, in reply to Mrs. Burke's observations concerning the ejection of the rector from the house which he occupied. She was good enough to spare my feelings by pointing out that from a business or legal point of view it was not I who was responsible for that act, but the parishioners, who, having purchased the rectory subject to a mortgage, had failed to meet the interest upon it. That is what Mrs.

189

Burke said: what she did not say, and what none of you have said in public, though I reckon you've said it among yourselves, I will take upon myself to say for her and you."

He paused—and every eye was fixed upon him and every mouth agape in paralysed astonishment: and the said features of Hepsey Burke were no exception to the rule.

"When," continued Bascom evenly and urbanely, "the word went round that the interest on the mortgage had got behind, and the money must be collected for it, those concerned no doubt remarked easily: 'Oh, I guess that'll be all right. Bascom won't worry about that; he don't need it; anyway he can pay it to himself, for the parish, if he does.'"

There was an uncomfortable stirring of the audience at this shrewd thrust; but Hepsey could not contain herself, and laughed right out, clapping loudly.

"And yet I don't mind saying that if I had thought of suggesting to anyone of you such a method of collecting interest due to you, you might have kicked some," he commented dryly.

"At the next step, when I ultimately concluded to act upon my right to eject Mr. Maxwell from the rectory, I've no doubt that on all sides it was: 'Well, did you ever know the likes of that? Turning the rector out of house and home! Well he's a skinflint for fair!'"

He paused and watched the effect. This time his hearers sat absolutely motionless.

"And I agree with you," he added presently, in a quiet voice: "I *was* a skinflint for fair!"

Almost Hepsey forgot herself so far as to clap thunderously: she caught her hands together just in time—recollecting that her demonstration would be taken too literally.

"But I would not have you misunderstand me: though it was for me to call myself a skinflint for that act, it was not for you to do so. You did so on wrong grounds. Those who in making money have been less successful than others, find it convenient to leave all such obligations upon the shoulders of the richer man, and to say 'it's up to him; he can afford it.' Is it any wonder that it makes the rich man sour on subscriptions and philanthropies? He has as much, or more, of inducement to apply his earnings and savings to his own ends and pleasures; why then, is it not up to all, in their own proportions to meet social needs? A good many years of such meanness among his neighbors makes even a rich man sour and mean, I guess. And that's what it made me—and though that isn't a justification of my act, it gave me as much right to call you skinflints as for you to call me: all except one of you, Hepsey Burke."

The meeting quivered with tense excitement. What did it all mean? If a chicken had sneezed the whole gathering would have been dissolved in hysterics, it was so keyed up with a sense of the impending disclosure of a deep mystery. As for Hepsey, she sat motionless, though Jonathan believed that he caught sight of a tear glistening in its descent.

"Hepsey Burke had a right to call me a skinflint, because she knew what none of you knew; but because it was private knowledge she wouldn't make use of it against me—not unless she couldn't have done what was right any other way. And now I'm going to tell you what she knew:

"The rectory was my wife's property, and she intended it as a gift to the parish, for the rectory of the church. I was preparing the deeds of transfer, when she died—suddenly, as some of you remember," his voice made heroic efforts to keep clear and steady, "owing to her death before the transfer, that house passed to our daughter; and what I intended to do was to buy it of her and present it to the parish. I delayed, at first for good reasons. And I suppose as I got more and more lonesome and mixed less and less with people, I got sourer—and then I delayed from meanness. It would have been easy enough for me to buy it of my daughter, and she'd have been willing enough; but as I saw more and more put upon me, and less and less human recognition—I was 'a rich man,' and needed no personal sympathy or encouragement, it seemed—I held back. And I got so mean, I couldn't make friends with the rector, even."

He paused, and from the half smile on his face, and the hint of brightness that passed over his expression, the audience caught relief.

"I guess a good shaking up is good for a man's liver: it cures a sour stomach—and as there are those that say the way to a man's heart is through his stomach, perhaps it cures a sour heart. I got my shaking up all right, as you know; and perhaps that's been working a cure on me. Or perhaps it was the quiet ministrations of that little Mrs. Betty of yours"—applause—"or the infusion of some of the rector's blood in my veins (he let himself be bled to keep me alive, after I'd lost what little blood I had, as you probably have never heard)"—shouts of applause—"or possibly what cured me was a little knitting-visit that Hepsey Burke paid me the other day, and during which she dropped some home-truths: I can't say.

"Before I decided what I would do about the rectory, I wanted to see what you would do, under Mrs. Burke's guidance, this evening. You've shouldered your share, as far as the rector's salary is concerned. Well—I'll add what I consider my fair share to that, fifty dollars. The arrears due on the mortgage interest is one hundred and twenty dollars. I shall hold you to your side of that bargain, to date. If you pay the rector the two hundred dollars due him on his salary, you will need to subscribe about another forty to make up the interest: that done, and paid to me, I will do my part, and present the rectory to the parish, in memory of my dear wife, as she desired."

He sat down.

Hepsey rose and called out in a clear voice:

"He's right; Mr. Bascom's dead right; it's up to us to be business first, and clear ourselves of the debt on a business bargain; then we can accept the gift without too much worryin'." And she sent a very friendly smile over to Bascom.

Again there was some cheering, in the midst of which Jonathan Jackson jumped to his feet beside Hepsey; and facing the room, with his arm through hers, he shouted:

"Hepsey Burke and me will make up the difference!"

Another cheer went up, and Hepsey's face flamed scarlet amid the craning of necks and chaffing laughter—half puzzled, half understanding.

Sylvester Bascom rose to his feet, and there was silence. With assumed seriousness he addressed Hepsey, still standing:

"Mrs. Burke, so that it may be quite in order, do you endorse Mr. Jackson's authority to speak for you in this matter?"

Every eye was turned upon them; but Hepsey could find not a word, so flabergasted was she by this sudden move of Jonathan's. Jonathan himself colored furiously, but stuck to his guns, and Hepsey's arm:

"Well, to tell the truth," he replied in a jaunty voice, "Hepsey Burke and me's goin' to be married right now, so I guess we'll combine our resources, like."

This announcement gave the coup de grace to any further attempt at orderliness, and the room became a seething chorus of congratulatory greetings aimed at Hepsey and Jonathan, in the midst of which Sylvester Bascom slipped out unnoticed.

CHAPTER XXIV
OMNIUM GATHERUM

When at last the room emptied, and she was free to do so, Hepsey, accompanied by the possessive Jonathan, found her way over to the Maxwells. Before she started to tell them the results of the meeting she cast a glance of whimsical affection at her palpitating fiance.

"I'd best let him get it off his chest—then we'll get down to business," she laughed.

So Jonathan, amid much handshaking and congratulation told his victorious story—until, when he seemed to Hepsey to become too triumphant, she broke in with: "Now that's enough for you, Mr. Proudmouth. Let me just say a word or two, will you? The meetin' wasn't called for you and me, and I want to tell about more important happenin's."

When they had heard of all that had been accomplished, Mrs. Betty got up and put her arms round Hepsey's neck and gave her such a hug, and a kiss on each cheek, that brought the tears to Mrs. Burke's eyes. And Donald, moist-eyed in spite of himself, took her hand in both of his, and expressed his feelings and relieved the tension at the same time by saying:

"Hepsey Burke, for all your molasses and the little bit of vinegar you say you keep by you, 'there are no flies on *you*' as Nickey would put it."

"HEPSEY BURKE, FOR ALL YOUR MOLASSES AND THE LITTLE
BIT OF VINEGAR YOU SAY YOU KEEP BY YOU, 'THERE ARE NO
FLIES ON YOU' AS NICKEY WOULD PUT IT"

At which sally Jonathan slapped his knee, and ejaculated:

"No! there 'aint, by gum! There 'aint no flies on Hepsey, if I *do* say it
myself."

At which proprietory speech Hepsey wagged her head warningly,
saying, as they left—"There's no downin' him, these days; I'm sure I
don't know what's come over the man."

On their way home Jonathan was urgent for fixing the day.

"You said you'd marry me right there and then, if the meetin' came
your way, now you know you did, Hepsey," he argued. "So if we
say to-morrow—"

But though Hepsey would never go back on a promise, she protested
against too summary an interpretation of it, and insisted on due time
to prepare herself for her wedding. So a day was set some two
months hence.

Meanwhile, Sylvester Bascom's truer and pristine nature blossomed
forth in the sunnier atmosphere around him, and after he had
delivered himself of his feelings to the Maxwells, in a visit which he
paid them next day at their nomadic quarters, he begged leave to put

the rectory in full repair before he handed it over to the parish, and the Maxwells returned to it.

And he was better than his word; for, with Hepsey and Virginia accompanying her, he insisted on Mrs. Betty taking a trip to the city a few days later for the purpose of selecting furnishings of various kinds dear to the hearts of housekeepers—Hepsey absorbing a share of the time in selecting her "trousseau."

Meanwhile, in due course the rectory was made a new place, inside and out, and a few weeks after their return the transformed house, repainted inside and out, papered and curtained and charmingly fitted with new furniture, was again occupied by the Maxwells.

That the interest of the parish should for a while be concentrated on the doings at the rectory, and diverted from her own important preparations, was a blessing to Hepsey—for she continually declared to Mrs. Betty that, little as she knew Jonathan in his new manner, she knew herself less!

It was decided that the wedding should be in the church, and a reception held after the ceremony, for the bride and bridegroom, at the rectory—and that, in this way, the whole parish would celebrate, in honor of the auspicious occasion, and of other happy results of Hepsey's parish meeting.

The day before the wedding, while Mrs. Betty and Virginia were busily occupied at Thunder Cliff and the rectory, dividing their attentions between the last touches to Hepsey's wardrobe, and preparing confections for the wedding guests, Donald Maxwell was closeted with Mr. Bascom at Willow Bluff for a considerable time. It was known that the Senior Warden was to support his colleague, Jonathan, at the morrow's event, and it was presumed that the rector was prompting him in his duties for the occasion.

The ceremony next day at the church was a center of fervent and cordial good-will and thanksgiving, as Jonathan, supported by Sylvester Bascom, took to wife Hepsey, given away by Mrs. Betty, with Virginia as a kind of maid of honor, hovering near. It was well for Donald Maxwell that his memory served him faithfully in conducting the service, for his eyes were in misty conflict with his bright smile. Nickey from the front pew, watched his mother with awestruck eyes, and with son-like amazement at her self-possessed carriage under the blaze of so much public attention.

There followed a procession from the church, and soon the rectory, house and garden, were alive with chattering groups, of all sorts and conditions, for the invitations had been general and public, irrespective of class or sect, at Hepsey's special request. There was a constant line of friends, known and unknown, filing past bride and bridegroom, with congratulatory greetings and cordial good wishes. There were speeches from delegations of various local bodies, and from local notables of various degrees; and there were wedding presents, out-vying each other, as it seemed, in kindly personal significance rather than in costliness. Among them all, and arranged by Mrs. Betty at the very center, the Vestry's gift to the bride stood easily first: a plated ice-water pitcher!

It was left to Maxwell to make the farewell speech, as the company crowded round the automobile, lent by the Bascoms, in which Hepsey and Jonathan sat in smiling happiness, ready to drive to the station, on their way for a week's honeymoon.

"Friends!" he said, in a voice that reached to the skirts of the assembled throng, "before we give a valedictory 'three times three' to the happy couple, I have to tell you of a plan that has been made to commemorate this day permanently—and so that Mrs. Jackson may not forget the place she holds in our hearts, and always will hold, as Hepsey Burke.

"It is Mr. Bascom's idea, and I know it will give lasting pleasure to Mrs. Burke—I mean Mrs. Jackson," he corrected, laughing, "as well as to all Durford, young and old. The beautiful piece of woodland, half a mile beyond Willow Bluff, is to-day presented by Mr. Bascom to the town, and we shall shortly repair there to watch the boys erect the tent now on the church plot, and which Mr. Jackson has kindly presented to the Boy Scouts."

"Gee," yelled Nickey, in astounded delight, and leading a cheer that interrupted the speaker for some moments.

Maxwell continued: "Mr. Bascom's generous gift to the town will be kept in order by the Boy Scouts, as their permanent camping-ground—and I daresay Nickey Burke will not be averse to occupying the tent with his corps, during the week or so that Mrs. Jackson is to be away. The place is to be called in her honor— 'Hepsey Burke Park.' And now—Three cheers for the bride and groom."

The cheers were given with whole-hearted fervor, as the man at the wheel tooted, and the auto started on its way with the smiling pair, followed by the people's delighted shouts of approbation at the happy plan for perpetuating among them the cheerful name of Hepsey Burke.

To The Reader

Being just a word or two
about ourselves

We are getting rather proud of the imprint which appears on the title pages and backs of all the books we publish. It is comparatively a new imprint, but the few years of our existence have been years of accomplishment.

Above all else we have aimed at publishing only a few books, but those few to be books that could be taken into the home,—our home or your home. In a word, the kind of books you want your daughters and your sons to read. Red-blooded and true as life is true, but clean.

If you have enjoyed this story and would like to become acquainted with other books which we publish fill out the following blank and in addition to our catalogue you will receive free of any charge a copy of:

A Little Journey to
The Home of Everywoman

By ELBERT HUBBARD

A pamphlet reprinted from the Philistine

Name ....

Address ....

Lightning Source UK Ltd.
Milton Keynes UK
UKHW040625170521
383859UK00001B/78